F. Scott Fitzgerald

The Curious Case of Benjamin Button

•

John Cheever

The Swimmer

martins
Martins Fontes

Publisher	*Evandro Mendonça Martins Fontes*
Coordenação editorial	*Anna Dantes*
Produção editorial	*Alyne Azuma*
Tradução	*Ana Luiza Couto*
Preparação	*Denise Roberti Camargo*
Revisão	*Beatriz Castro Nunes de Souza*
	Dinarte Zorzanelli da Silva
Biografias e apresentações	*Laura Fernández*
Locução de "The Curious (...) Button"	*David Tamke*
Locução de "The Swimmer"	*David Tamke*
Gravação	*RecLab*
Técnico	*Francesc Gosalves*

Dados Internacionais de Catalogação na Publicação (CIP)
(Câmara Brasileira do Livro, SP, Brasil)

Fitzgerald, F. Scott, 1869-1940.

The curious case of Benjamin Button / F. Scott Fitzgerald. The Swimmer / John Cheever ; [traduzido por Ana Luiza Couto]. -- São Paulo : Martins Martins Fontes, 2011.

Título original: The curious case of Benjamin Button ; The Swimmer

Inclui CD.

ISBN 978-85-8063-005-3

1. Ficção norte-americana I. Cheever, John. II. Título. III. Título: The swimmer.

11-01737 CDD-813

Índices para catálogo sistemático:

1. Ficção : Literatura norte-americana 813

Av. Dr. Arnaldo, 2076
01255-000 São Paulo SP Brasil
Tel. (11) 3116.0000
info@martinseditora.com.br
www.martinsmartinsfontes.com.br

SUMÁRIO

INTRODUÇÃO

Dê um passo além e leia os clássicos em versão original

Para muitos de nós, ler em versão original supõe um desafio por vezes irrealizável. Habituados a nossa própria língua, ficamos frustrados quando não entendemos todas as palavras de um texto. Quantas vezes deixamos um livro de lado porque não queremos consultar o dicionário a toda hora? Essa consulta (quase sempre obrigatória) se soma ao desconhecimento das referências culturais, à dificuldade de perceber os matizes, a ironia do autor etc. Logo nos aborrecemos por não conseguir compreender a essência do relato e acabamos fechando o livro e buscando a versão traduzida.

Na coleção READ & LISTEN a leitura e audição do texto original produzem experiências tão únicas quanto a de contemplar uma pintura em vez de sua reprodução. Não só se aprende como também se desfruta e assimila o verdadeiro espírito do relato.

Aqui, os leitores podem ter acesso aos melhores contos dos mais respeitados autores de língua inglesa, com as ferramentas necessárias para compreender os textos em sua totalidade.

Foi-se o tempo de ler com o dicionário do lado. Cada conto inclui um extenso glossário para que não seja necessário interromper a leitura. Além de todas as palavras que você pode não entender, ele apresenta referências culturais, deixa claras as nuances e permite compreender todos os toques irônicos de cada conto. Para quem quer praticar a compreensão oral ou simplesmente ouvir o texto enquanto o lê, nada mais simples. Ponha o CD com a versão em áudio dos contos para tocar, sente-se, relaxe e deixe que um locutor nativo conte a história. Porque não há maneira melhor de colocar ao seu alcance essas obras-primas do que rompendo as barreiras que o mantiveram longe delas durante tanto tempo.

Quem tem medo dos clássicos?

E por falar em clássicos... Nossa seleção se guiou por várias premissas: em primeiro lugar, os contos tinham de ser sugestivos e não muito complexos; em segundo lugar, tinham de representar o mundo próprio de cada autor. Clássicos em miniatura, inesquecíveis, os contos desta coleção devem ser lidos com cuidado, degustando cada frase, cada palavra. São obras capazes de transformar seus personagens em alguém conhecido, quase familiar, que poderia ser seu melhor amigo.

Acreditamos que, depois de tanto tempo aprendendo inglês, chegou seu momento de desfrutar. Você merece.

F. Scott Fitzgerald

The Curious Case of Benjamin Button

"Blind with enchantment, he felt that life was just beginning."

BIOGRAFIA

F. Scott Fitzgerald

Francis Scott Fitzgerald é, com William Faulkner e Ernest Hemingway, um dos membros mais destacados da chamada Geração Perdida (formada pelos escritores norte-americanos nascidos no final do século XIX que tiveram de conviver, em sua juventude, com a Primeira Guerra Mundial). Nascido em Saint Paul, Minnesota, em 1896, Scott Fitzgerald sempre soube que queria ser escritor. Por isso, quando estourou a Grande Guerra escreveu às pressas seu primeiro romance, *The Romantic Egotist*, e se alistou no exército (por volta de 1917, quando tinha 21 anos). Terminou a guerra num acampamento militar acreditando que morreria no *front* e se converteria num clássico instantâneo. Por sorte, a guerra acabou antes que fosse enviado para a luta.

Num dos acampamentos conheceu Zelda Sayre, a garota pela qual era capaz de cruzar o país numa sucata sobre rodas (como costumavam chamar seu velho Marmon de segunda mão) e com quem acabou se casando em 1920, uma semana depois de a versão revista de *The Romantic Egotist*, publicada no Brasil como *Este lado do paraíso*, se converter num sucesso de vendas. Até então, Scott Fitzgerald havia se dedicado à publicidade e a escrever contos que vendia a revistas de todo tipo (incluindo automobilísticas) e teve de continuar fazendo isso porque Zelda se recusou a trabalhar, e seu estilo de vida esbanjador converteu Scott Fitzgerald num incansável contista.

Publicado em 1922, seu segundo romance, *Os belos e malditos*, nutre-se desses primeiros anos com Zelda e assenta as bases do desencanto existencial que marcou sua vida e sua obra. Durante a década de 1920, Fitzgerald se converteu num clássico vivo (*O Grande Gatsby* foi publicado em 1925), viajou para a Europa, fez amizade com Hemingway e pareceu ter retomado as rédeas de seu descontrolado e doentio cotidiano. Mas era apenas uma ilusão. Em 1930, Zelda foi internada num hospital psiquiátrico, com esquizofrenia. As contas do hospital se somam às do colégio de sua única filha (que o casal abandonou desde cedo) e às garrafas de uísque acumuladas na despensa. Scott Fitzgerald consegue terminar seu quarto romance, *Suave é a noite*, mas precisa se lançar aos braços de Hollywood e escrever comédias para chegar ao fim do mês. Ainda assim, segue escrevendo contos nos quais se sucedem relações atormentadas entre homens que sabem demais e moças bonitas cheias de segundas intenções.

Sua necessidade tardia de escrever roteiros cinematográficos o obrigou a se mudar para Hollywood, onde conheceu Sheilah Graham, uma admiradora disposta a tirá-lo do buraco e que nunca foi mais do que uma sombra da caprichosa e desequilibrada Zelda. Enquanto escrevia seu último romance, *O último magnata*, sempre embriagado, sofreu um ataque cardíaco fulminante. Era 1940, e ele acabava de completar 44 anos. Não completaria mais um. Oito anos depois foi a vez de Zelda, que morreu num incêndio no hospital psiquiátrico em que estava internada. Tinha 47 anos.

LAURA FERNÁNDEZ

APRESENTAÇÃO DO CONTO
The Curious Case of Benjamin Button

Por volta de 1860, o Hospital Particular para Damas e Cavalheiros de Maryland foi testemunha do nascimento de um senhor de 70 anos. Assim, do nada. Um senhor de 70 anos que, quando viu o pai, pediu-lhe uma bengala. Depois pediu um traje adequado a um senhor de 70 anos. "Não pretende que eu saia daqui enrolado numa manta?", perguntou o velho bebê, que, com certeza, tinha o cabelo branco. Assim, o pai, um sujeito chamado Roger Button, a quem até então a vida havia sorrido, não teve outro remédio senão confundir o empregado de uma loja de roupas para bebê. "O senhor não acaba de dizer que seu filho tem seis horas de vida?", pergunta o atendente quando descobre Roger despindo um manequim vestido com o que parece ser uma roupa de mosqueteiro. "Na realidade quis dizer dezesseis anos", responde Button. "Qual vai ser o meu nome, papai?", pergunta o velho recém-nascido na saída do hospital, ao que Roger responde: "Não sei, acho que Matusalém".

Assim começa "The Curious Case of Benjamin Button", a história do único bebê do mundo que, em vez de fazer anos, os *desfaz*. A cada dia que passa Benjamin (nome com que afinal batizaram o velho) fica um pouco mais jovem. As rugas se esticam, o cabelo se torna mais forte e mais negro (pouco a pouco vai abandonando a tinta que seu pai o obrigava a usar desde o nascimento) e seus conhecimentos diminuem. Assim, se casa quando tem apenas 18 anos (mas aparenta 50) e começa a universidade aos 57 (quando aparenta 23). Se de início se dá bem com seu avô (e mantém longas conversas com ele na cadeira de balanço), depois começa a se dar melhor com seu pai (chega o dia em que parecem irmãos) e com certeza chega o momento em que seu filho Roscoe parece ter o dobro da sua idade.

"The Curious Case of Benjamin Button" foi publicado pela primeira vez na revista *Collier's*, em 1921, e depois fez parte da antologia *Tales of the Jazz Age*, sempre ocupando o lugar mais destacado (muitas vezes essa mesma antologia recebia o título de *The Curious Case of Benjamin Button and Other Jazz Age Stories*), já que sempre foi considerado seu melhor conto. Escrito de maneira simples, quase infantil, à moda de uma fábula para adultos, o leitor iniciado poderá desfrutar a história de um homem que viveu na contracorrente (o bebê que nasceu velho é um brutal exemplo do diferente, do que não se encaixa) e recorrer ao glossário para resolver as dúvidas. Para aqueles que quiserem praticar a pronúncia ou desfrutar sua compreensão, nada melhor do que emprestar os ouvidos à versão em áudio do conto que está no CD.

Prepare-se, pois, para submergir no caminho de volta de Benjamin Button ao berço do qual quis sair quando nasceu por achá-lo, naquele momento, muito incômodo para seus ossos maltratados. Um caminho de volta que funciona como alegoria da vida do autor, um homem que acreditou que o dinheiro e a juventude fossem eternos e que se acostumou a viver à margem de uma sociedade que lhe permitiu tudo em troca do vazio existencial, "The Curious Case of Benjamin Button" é, definitivamente, uma pequena obra-prima do desencanto, uma espécie de ode à vida que não escolhemos.

LAURA FERNÁNDEZ

The Curious Case of Benjamin Button

I

As LONG AGO AS 1860 it was the proper thing to be born at home. At present, so I am told, the high gods of medicine have decreed[1] that the first cries[2] of the young shall be uttered[3] upon the anaesthetic air of a hospital, preferably a fashionable one. So young Mr. and Mrs. Roger Button were fifty years ahead of style when they decided, one day in the summer of 1860, that their first baby should be born in a hospital. Whether this anachronism had any bearing[4] upon the astonishing history I am about to set down[5] will never be known.

I shall tell you what occurred, and let you judge for yourself.

The Roger Buttons held an enviable position, both social and financial, in ante-bellum Baltimore[6]. They were related to the This Family and the That Family, which, as every Southerner knew, entitled them to membership in that enormous peerage[7] which largely populated the Confederacy[8].

1 **have decreed:** decretaram • 2 **the first cries:** o primeiro choro • 3 **shall be uttered:** deve acontecer • 4 **had any bearing:** tinha algo a ver • 5 **about to set down:** me apresso a registrar • 6 **ante-bellum Baltimore:** a cidade de Baltimore antes da Guerra Civil (1861-1865) • 7 **peerage:** aristocracia • 8 **Confederacy:** Confederados (nome dados aos Estados do sul, cuja intenção de se separar da Federação significou o início da Guerra Civil)

This was their first experience with the charming old custom of having babies—Mr. Button was naturally nervous. He hoped it would be a boy so that he could be sent to Yale College in Connecticut, at which institution Mr. Button himself had been known for four years by the somewhat obvious nickname[1] of "Cuff[2]".

On the September morning consecrated to the enormous event he arose[3] nervously at six o'clock, dressed himself, adjusted an impecable stock[4], and hurried forth[5] through the streets of Baltimore to the hospital, to determine whether[6] the darkness of the night had borne in new life upon its bosom[7].

When he was approximately a hundred yards[8] from the Maryland Private Hospital for Ladies and Gentlemen he saw Doctor Keene, the family physician[9], descending the front steps, rubbing his hands together[10] with a washing movement—as all doctors are required to do by the unwritten ethics of their profession.

Mr. Roger Button, the president of Roger Button & Co., Wholesale Hardware[11], began to run toward Doctor Keene with much less dignity than was expected from a Southern gentleman of that picturesque period. "Doctor Keene!" he called. "Oh, Doctor Keene!"

The doctor heard him, faced around[12], and stood waiting,

1 **nickname:** apelido • 2 **cuff:** punho de camisa (provavelmente uma brincadeira com seu próprio nome, "button", que significa botão) • 3 **he arose:** se levantou • 4 **adjusted an impeccable stock:** deu um nó impecável na gravata • 5 **hurried forth:** correu • 6 **whether:** se • 7 **bosom:** seio • 8 **yard:** jarda (0,91 m) • 9 **physician:** médico (forma antiga) • 10 **rubbing his hands together:** esfregando as mãos • 11 **Wholesale Hardware:** Atacado de Ferramentas • 12 **faced around:** se voltou

a curious expression settling on his harsh[1], medicinal face as Mr. Button drew near[2].

"What happened?" demanded Mr. Button, as he came up in a gasping rush[3]. "What was it? How is she? A boy? Who is it? What——"

"Talk sense!" said Doctor Keene sharply. He appeared somewhat irritated.

"Is the child born?" begged Mr. Button.

Doctor Keene frowned[4]. "Why, yes, I suppose so—after a fashion[5]." Again he threw a curious glance at Mr. Button[6].

"Is my wife all right?"

"Yes."

"Is it a boy or a girl?"

"Here now[7]!" cried Doctor Keene in a perfect passion of irritation[8], "I'll ask you to go and see for yourself[9]. Outrageous[10]!" He snapped[11] the last word out in almost one syllable, then he turned away muttering[12]: "Do you imagine a case like this will help my professional reputation? One more would ruin[13] me—ruin anybody."

"What's the matter?" demanded Mr. Button appalled[14]. "Triplets[15]?"

"No, not triplets!" answered the doctor cuttingly[16]. "What's

1 **harsh:** dura • 2 **drew near:** se aproximava • 3 **in a gasping rush:** ofegante pela corrida • 4 **frowned:** franziu o cenho • 5 **after a fashion:** de certa forma • 6 **he threw a furious glance at Mr. Button:** lançou um estranho olhar ao sr. Button • 7 **here now!:** Essa agora! • 8 **in a perfect passion of irritation:** absolutamente irritado • 9 **see for yourself:** veja você mesmo • 10 **outrageous:** ultrajante • 11 **he snapped:** disse com rispidez • 12 **muttering:** resmungando • 13 **ruin:** arruinaria • 14 **appalled:** apavorado • 15 **triplets:** trigêmeos • 16 **cuttingly:** de forma cortante

more, you can go and see for yourself. And get another doctor. I brought you into the world, young man, and I've been physician to your family for forty years, but I'm through with you[1]! I don't want to see you or any of your relatives[2] ever again! Good-by!"

Then he turned sharply[3], and without another word climbed into his phaeton[4], which was waiting at the curbstone[5], and drove severely away.

Mr. Button stood there upon the sidewalk, stupefied and trembling from head to foot. What horrible mishap[6] had occurred? He had suddenly lost all desire to go into the Maryland Private Hospital for Ladies and Gentlemen—it was with the greatest difficulty that, a moment later, he forced himself to mount the steps[7] and enter the front door.

A nurse was sitting behind a desk in the opaque gloom[8] of the hall. Swallowing his shame[9], Mr. Button approached her.

"Good-morning," she remarked, looking up at him pleasantly.

"Good-morning. I—I am Mr. Button."

At this a look of utter[10] terror spread itself over girl's face. She rose to her feet[11] and seemed about to fly from the hall, restraining herself[12] only with the most apparent difficulty.

"I want to see my child," said Mr. Button.

1 **I'm through with you:** agora acabou • 2 **relatives:** parentes • 3 **he turned sharply:** se voltou bruscamente • 4 **phaeton:** faeton; faetonte (tipo de carruagem) • 5 **curbstone:** meio-fio • 6 **mishap:** desgraça • 7 **to mount the steps:** subir os degraus • 8 **opaque gloom:** sombra opaca • 9 **swallowing his shame:** engolindo sua vergonha • 10 **utter:** total, absoluto • 11 **she rose to her feet:** se levantou • 12 **restraining herself:** se contendo

The nurse gave a little scream. "Oh—of course!" she cried hysterically. "Up-stairs. Right up-stairs. Go—*up*!"

She pointed the direction, and Mr. Button, bathed in cool perspiration[1], turned falteringly[2], and began to mount to the second floor. In the upper hall he addressed another nurse who approached him, basin[3] in hand. "I'm Mr. Button," he managed to articulate. "I want to see my—"

Clank! The basin clattered to the floor[4] and rolled[5] in the direction of the stairs. Clank! Clank! It began a methodical decent as if sharing in the general terror which this gentleman provoked.

"I want to see my child!" Mr. Button almost shrieked[6]. He was on the verge of collapse.

Clank! The basin reached the first floor. The nurse regained control of herself[7], and threw Mr. Button a look of hearty contempt[8].

"All *right*, Mr. Button," she agreed in a hushed[9] voice. "Very *well!* But if you *knew* what state it's put us all in this morning! It's perfectly outrageous! The hospital will never have the ghost of[10] a reputation after—"

"Hurry!" he cried hoarsely[11]. "I can't stand this!"

"Come this way, then, Mr. Button."

He dragged himself after her[12]. At the end of a long hall

1 **perspiration:** suor • 2 **turned falteringly:** se virou balbuciando • 3 **basin:** bacia • 4 **clattered to the floor:** tiniu contra o solo • 5 **rolled:** rolou • 6 **shrieked:** gritou • 7 **the nurse regained control of herself:** a enfermeira recuperou a compostura • 8 **threw Mr. Button a look of hearty contempt:** lançou ao sr. Button um olhar cheio de desprezo • 9 **hushed:** abafada • 10 **a ghost of:** nem um vislumbre de • 11 **hoarsely:** com a voz partida • 12 **he dragged himself after her:** a seguiu a contragosto

they reached a room from which proceeded a variety of howls[1]—indeed, a room which, in later parlance, would have been known as the "crying-room." They entered. Ranged around the walls were half a dozen white-enameled rolling cribs[2], each with a tag[3] tied at the head.

"Well," gasped Mr. Button, "which is mine?"

"There!" said the nurse.

Mr. Button's eyes followed her pointing finger, and this is what he saw. Wrapped[4] in a voluminous white blanket, and partly crammed[5] into one of the cribs, there sat an old man apparently about seventy years of age. His sparse[6] hair was almost white, and from his chin[7] dripped a long smoke-colored beard[8], which waved absurdly back and forth, fanned by the breeze coming in at the window[9]. He looked up at Mr. Button with dim, faded eyes[10] in which lurked[11] a puzzled question[12].

"Am I mad?" thundered Mr. Button, his terror resolving into rage. "Is this some ghastly[13] hospital joke?

"It doesn't seem like a joke to us," replied the nurse severely. "And I don't know whether you're mad or not—but that is most certainly your child."

The cool perspiration redoubled[14] on Mr. Button's forehead[15]. He closed his eyes, and then, opening them, looked

1 **howls:** berros • 2 **white-enameled rolling cribs:** berços esmaltados de branco com rodas • 3 **tag:** etiqueta • 4 **wrapped:** enrolado • 5 **crammed:** comprimido • 6 **sparse:** ralo • 7 **chin:** queixo • 8 **a long smoke-colored beard:** uma longa barba cor de fumaça • 9 **fanned by the breeze coming in at the window:** movida pela brisa que entrava pela janela • 10 **dim, faded eyes:** os olhos enevoados e apagados • 11 **lurked:** se escondia • 12 **a puzzled question:** uma pergunta desconcertante • 13 **ghastly:** macabra • 14 **redoubled:** se intensificou • 15 **forehead:** testa

again. There was no mistake—he was gazing at[1] a man of threescore and ten[2]—a *baby* of threescore and ten, a baby whose feet hung over the sides of the crib in which it was reposing.

The old man looked placidly from one to the other for a moment, and then suddenly spoke in a cracked[3] and ancient voice. "Are you my father?" he demanded.

Mr. Button and the nurse started violently.

"Because if you are," went on the old man querulously[4], "I wish you'd get me out of this place—or, at least, get them to put a comfortable rocker[5] in here,"

"Where in God's name did you come from? Who are you?" burst out[6] Mr. Button frantically[7].

"I can't tell you *exactly* who I am," replied the querulous whine[8], "because I've only been born a few hours—but my last name is certainly Button."

"You lie! You're an impostor!"

The old man turned wearily[9] to the nurse. "Nice way to welcome a new-born child," he complained in a weak voice. "Tell him he's wrong, why don't you?"

"You're wrong. Mr. Button," said the nurse severely. "This is your child, and you'll have to make the best of it. We're going to ask you to take him home with you as soon as possible—some time today."

"Home?" repeated Mr. Button incredulously.

1 **gazing at:** contemplando • 2 **threescore and ten:** 70 (forma antiga) • 3 **cracked:** alquebrada • 4 **querulously:** de modo rabugento • 5 **get them to put a comfortable rocker:** faça que coloquem aqui uma cadeira de balanço confortável • 6 **burst out:** exclamou • 7 **frantically:** desesperado • 8 **the querulous whine:** um gemido ranzinza • 9 **wearily:** com cansaço

"Yes, we can't have him here. We really can't, you know?"

"I'm right glad of it," whined[1] the old man. "This is a fine place to keep a youngster of quiet tastes. With all this yelling and howling[2], I haven't been able to get a wink of sleep. I asked for something to eat"—here his voice rose to a shrill note of protest—"and they brought me a bottle of milk!"

Mr. Button, sank down upon a chair[3] near his son and concealed[4] his face in his hands. "My heavens!" he murmured, in an ecstasy of horror. "What will people say? What must I do?"

"You'll have to take him home," insisted the nurse —"immediately!"

A grotesque picture formed itself with dreadful clarity before the eyes of the tortured man—a picture of himself walking through the crowded streets of the city with this appalling[5] apparition stalking[6] by his side. "I can't. I can't," he moaned[7].

People would stop to speak to him, and what was he going to say? He would have to introduce this—this septuagenarian: "This is my son, born early this morning." And then the old man would gather his blanket around him[8] and they would plod on[9], past the bustling stores[10], the slave market[11]—

1 **whined:** queixou-se • 2 **with all this yelling and howling:** com toda esta gritaria 3 **sank down upon a chair:** se afundou numa cadeira • 4 **concealed:** escondeu • 5 **appalling:** espantosa • 6 **stalking:** andando • 7 **he moaned:** lamentou-se • 8 **the old man would gather his blanket around him:** o velhinho se enrolaria em seu cobertor • 9 **they would plod on:** caminhariam lentamente • 10 **the bustling stores:** as lojas agitadas • 11 **the slave market:** o mercado de escravos

for a dark instant Mr. Button wished passionately that his son was black—past the luxurious houses of the residential district, past the home for the aged[1]. . . .

"Come! Pull yourself together[2]," commanded[3] the nurse.

"See here," the old man announced suddenly[4], "if you think I'm going to walk home in this blanket, you're entirely mistaken."

"Babies always have blankets."

With a malicious crackle[5] the old man held up a small white swaddling garment[6]. "Look!" he quavered[7]. "*This* is what they had ready for me."

"Babies always wear those," said the nurse primly[8].

"Well," said the old man, "this baby's not going to wear anything in about two minutes. This blanket itches[9]. They might at least have given me a sheet."

"Keep it on[10]! Keep it on!" said Mr. Button hurriedly. He turned to the nurse. "What'll I do[11]?"

"Go down town and buy your son some clothes."

Mr. Button's son's voice followed him down into the hall: "And a cane[12], father. I want to have a cane."

Mr. Button banged the outer door savagely[13]. . . .

1 **the aged:** os idosos • 2 **pull yourself together:** controle-se • 3 **commanded:** ordenou • 4 **suddenly:** de repente • 5 **crackle:** risada • 6 **swaddling garment:** fraldas • 7 **he quavered:** disse com a voz trêmula • 8 **primly:** num tom formal • 9 **this blanket itches:** este cobertor coça • 10 **keep it on!:** não o tire! • 11 **what'll I do? (what shall I do?):** O que eu devo fazer? • 12 **cane:** bengala • 13 **banged the outer door savagely:** fechou a porta com brutalidade

II

"Good-morning," Mr. Button said, nervously, to the clerk[1] in the Chesapeake Dry Goods Company. "I want to buy some clothes for my child."

"How old is your child, sir?"

"About six hours," answered Mr. Button, without due consideration[2].

"Babies' supply department in the rear[3]."

"Why, I don't think—I'm not sure that's what I want. It's—he's an unusually large-size child. Exceptionally—ah—large."

"They have the largest child's sizes."

"Where is the boys' department?" inquired[4] Mr. Button, shifting his ground desperately[5]. He felt that the clerk must surely scent his shameful secret[6].

"Right here."

"Well—" He hesitated. The notion of dressing his son in men's clothes was repugnant to him. If, say, he could only find a *very* large boy's suit, he might cut off that long and awful beard[7], dye[8] the white hair brown, and thus manage to conceal the worst, and to retain[9] something of his own self-respect—not to mention his position in Baltimore society.

1 **clerk:** balconista • 2 **without due consideration:** sem pensar • 3 **in the rear:** nos fundos • 4 **inquired:** perguntou • 5 **shifting his ground desperately:** mudando de posição, agoniado • 6 **the clerk must surely scent his shameful secret:** o balconista devia estar intuindo o seu segredo vergonhoso • 7 **he might cut off that long and awful beard:** podia cortar aquela barba comprida e horrorosa • 8 **dye:** tingir • 9 **to retain:** conservar

But a frantic[1] inspection of the boys' department revealed no suits to fit[2] the new-born Button. He blamed the store[3], of course—in such cases it is the thing[4] to blame the store.

"How old did you say that boy of yours was?" demanded the clerk curiously.

"He's—sixteen."

"Oh, I beg your pardon. I thought you said six *hours*. You'll find the youths' department in the next aisle[5]."

Mr. Button turned miserably away. Then he stopped, brightened, and pointed his finger toward a dressed dummy[6] in the window display. "There!" he exclaimed. "I'll take that suit, out there on the dummy."

The clerk stared[7]. "Why," he protested, "that's not a child's suit. At least it *is*, but it's for fancy dress[8]. You could wear it yourself!"

"Wrap it up[9]," insisted his customer nervously.

"That's what I want."

The astonished[10] clerk obeyed.

Back at the hospital[11] Mr. Button entered the nursery[12] and almost threw the package[13] at his son. "Here's your clothes," he snapped out[14].

The old man untied[15] the package and viewed the contents with a quizzical eye[16].

1 **frantic:** frenética • 2 **to fit:** que servissem • 3 **store:** loja • 4 **it is the thing:** o normal é • 5 **aisle:** corredor • 6 **dummy:** manequim • 7 **stared**: olhou-o fixamente • 8 **fancy dress:** fantasia • 9 **wrap it up:** embrulhe-o • 10 **astonished:** atônito • 11 **back at the hospital:** de volta ao hospital • 12 **nursery:** berçário • 13 **almost threw the package:** praticamente atirou o pacote • 14 **he snapped out:** disse bruscamente • 15 **untied:** desatou; abriu • 16 **with a quizzical eye:** com um olhar zombeteiro

"They look sort of funny to me[1]," he complained, "I don't want to be made a monkey of[2]——"

"You've made a monkey of me!" retorted[3] Mr. Button fiercely. "Never you mind how funny you look. Put them on—or I'll—or I'll *spank* you[4]." He swallowed uneasily[5] at the penultimate word, feeling nevertheless that it was the proper thing to say.

"All right, father"—this with a grotesque simulation of filial respect—"you've lived longer; you know best. Just as you say."

As before, the sound of the word "father" caused Mr. Button to start[6] violently.

"And hurry."

"I'm hurrying, father."

When his son was dressed Mr. Button regarded him with depression. The costume consisted of dotted socks[7], pink pants[8], and a belted blouse[9] with a wide white collar. Over the latter waved the long whitish beard, drooping almost to the waist[10]. The effect was not good.

"Wait!"

Mr. Button seized a hospital shears[11] and with three quick snaps[12] amputated a large section of the beard. But even with

1 **they look sort of funny to me:** me parecem um pouco esquisitas • 2 **I don't want to be made a monkey of:** não quero que riam de mim • 3 **retorted:** replicou • 4 **I'll spank you:** vou lhe dar um tapa • 5 **swallowed uneasily:** engoliu em seco • 6 **to start:** se sobressaltar • 7 **dotted socks:** meias com pintinhas • 8 **pink pants:** calças cor-de-rosa • 9 **a belted blouse:** uma blusa com uma faixa na cintura • 10 **drooping almost to the waist:** chegando quase até a cintura • 11 **Mr. Button seized a hospital shears:** o sr. Button pegou uma tesoura do hospital • 12 **snaps:** tesouradas

this improvement the ensemble fell far short of perfection[1]. The remaining brush of scraggly hair[2]; the watery eyes, the ancient teeth, seemed oddly out of tone with the gaiety[3] of the costume. Mr. Button, however, was obdurate[4]—he held out his hand. "Come along!" he said sternly[5].

His son took the hand trustingly. "What are you going to call me, dad?" he quavered[6] as they walked from the nursery—"just 'baby' for a while? till you think of a better name?"

Mr. Button grunted[7]. "I don't know," he answered harshly[8]. "I think we'll call you Methuselah[9]."

III

Even after the new addition to the Button family had had his hair cut short and then dyed to a sparse unnatural black, had had his face shaved so dose that it glistened[10], and had been attired[11] in small-boy clothes made to order[12] by a flabbergasted[13] tailor, it was impossible for Mr. Button to ignore the fact that his son was a poor excuse[14] for a first family baby. Despite his aged stoop[15], Benjamin Button—for it was by

1 **the ensemble fell far short of perfection:** o conjunto estava muito longe da perfeição • 2 **brush of scraggly hair:** tufo de cabelo despenteado • 3 **gaiety:** colorido • 4 **obdurate:** obstinado • 5 **sternly:** de modo autoritário • 6 **he quavered:** perguntou ele com voz trêmula • 7 **grunted:** grunhiu • 8 **harshly:** asperamente • 9 **Methuselah:** Matusalém • 10 **had had his face shaved so close that it glistened:** lhe fizeram tanto a barba que seu rosto brilhava • 11 **attired:** vestido (formal) • 12 **made to order:** feitas sob medida• 13 **flabbergastered:** atônito • 14 **a poor excuse:** uma desculpa insatisfatória • 15 **his aged stoop:** sua postura encurvada

this name they called him instead of by the appropriate but invidious[1] Methuselah—was five feet eight inches tall[2]. His clothes did not conceal this, nor did the clipping[3] and dyeing[4] of his eyebrows disguise the fact that the eyes underneath were faded and watery and tired. In fact, the baby-nurse who had been engaged in advance[5] left the house after one look, in a state of considerable indignation.

But Mr. Button persisted in his unwavering purpose[6]. Benjamin was a baby, and a baby he should remain. At first he declared that if Benjamin didn't like warm milk he could go without food altogether, but he was finally prevailed upon[7] to allow his son bread and butter, and even oatmeal[8] by way of a compromise[9]. One day he brought home a rattle[10] and, giving it to Benjamin, insisted in no uncertain terms[11] that he should "play with it," whereupon[12] the old man took it with a weary[13] expression and could be heard jingling[14] it obediently at intervals throughout the day.

There can be no doubt, though, that the rattle bored him, and that he found other and more soothing amusements[15] when he was left alone. For instance, Mr. Button discovered one day that during the preceding week be had smoked more cigars[16] than ever before—a phenomenon, which

1 **invidious:** ofensivo • 2 **five feet eight inches:** 1,72 m • 3 **clipping:** corte • 4 **dyeing:** tintura • 5 **engaged in advance:** contratada com antecedência • 6 **unwavering purpose:** férrea determinação • 7 **he was prevailed upon:** cedeu • 8 **oatmeal:** mingau de aveia • 9 **by way of a compromise:** de comum acordo • 10 **rattle:** chocalho • 11 **in no uncertain terms:** de forma taxativa • 12 **whereupon:** e em consequência disso • 13 **weary:** cansada • 14 **jingling:** chacoalhando • 15 **more soothing amusements:** passatempos mais amenos • 16 **cigars:** charutos

was explained a few days later when, entering the nursery unexpectedly, he found the room full of faint blue haze[1] and Benjamin, with a guilty expression on his face, trying to conceal the butt[2] of a dark Havana. This, of course, called for[3] a severe spanking, but Mr. Button found that he could not bring himself to administer it. He merely[4] warned his son that he would "stunt his growth[5]."

Nevertheless he persisted in his attitude. He brought home lead soldiers[6], he brought toy trains, he brought large pleasant animals made of cotton, and, to perfect the illusion which he was creating—for himself at least—he passionately demanded of the clerk in the toy-store whether "the paint would come off the pink duck if the baby put it in his mouth." But, despite all his father's efforts, Benjamin refused to be interested. He would steal down the back stairs[7] and return to the nursery with a volume of the "Encyclopaedia Britannica", over which he would pore[8] through an afternoon, while his cotton cows and his Noah's ark were left neglected on the floor. Against such a stubborness[9] Mr. Button's efforts were of little avail[10].

The sensation created in Baltimore was, at first, prodigious. What the mishap would have cost the Buttons and their kinsfolk[11] socially cannot be determined, for the outbreak of the Civil War[12] drew the city's attention to other

1 **faint blue haze:** tênue neblina azul • 2 **butt:** guimba • 3 **called for:** merecia • 4 **merely:** simplesmente • 5 **stunt his growth:** atrapalhar seu crescimento • 6 **lead soldiers:** soldadinhos de chumbo • 7 **he would steal down the back stairs:** escapulia pela escada dos fundos • 8 **over which we would pore:** no qual mergulhava • 9 **stubbornness:** obstinação • 10 **of little avail:** de pouca valia • 11 **kinsfolk:** parentes • 12 **the outbreak of the Civil War:** a deflagração da Guerra Civil

things. A few people who were unfailingly polite[1] racked their brains[2] for compliments to give to the parents—and finally hit upon the ingenious device of declaring that the baby resembled his grandfather, a fact which, due to the standard state of decay common to all men of seventy, could not be denied. Mr. and Mrs. Roger Button were not pleased, and Benjamin's grandfather was furiously insulted.

Benjamin, once he left the hospital, took life as he found it. Several small boys were brought to see him, and he spent a stiff-jointed afternoon[3] trying to work up an interest[4] in tops and marbles[5]—he even managed, quite accidentally, to break a kitchen window with a stone from a sling shot[6], a feat[7] which secretly delighted his father.

Thereafter[8] Benjamin contrived to break[9] something every day, but he did these things only because they were expected of him, and because he was by nature obliging[10].

When his grandfather's initial antagonism wore off[11], Benjamin and that gentleman took enormous pleasure in one another's company. They would sit for hours, these two, so far apart in age and experience, and, like old cronies[12], discuss with tireless[13] monotony the slow events of the day.

1 **unfailingly polite:** escrupulosamente educados • 2 **racked their brains:** quebravam a cabeça • 3 **a stiff-jointed afternoon:** uma tarde difícil • 4 **trying to work up an interest:** tentando demonstrar interesse • 5 **tops and marbles:** piões e bolinhas de gude • 6 **sling shot:** estilingue • 7 **feat:** façanha • 8 **thereafter:** desde então • 9 **contrived to break:** se programou para quebrar • 10 **obliging:** prestativo • 11 **when his grandfather's initial antagonism wore off:** quando o antagonismo inicial de seu avô passou • 12 **old cronies:** velhos companheiros • 13 **tireless:** incansável

Benjamin felt more at ease[1] in his grandfather's presence than in his parents'—they seemed always somewhat in awe of him[2] and, despite the dictatorial authority they exercised over him, frequently addressed him as "Mr."

He was as puzzled[3] as any one else at the apparently advanced age of his mind and body at birth. He read up on it in the medical journal[4], but found that no such case had been previously recorded. At his father's urging[5] he made an honest attempt to play with other boys, and frequently he joined in the milder games[6]—football[7] shook him up too much, and he feared that in case of a fracture his ancient bones would refuse to knit[8].

When he was five he was sent to kindergarten[9], where he was initiated into the art of pasting[10] green paper on orange paper, of weaving[11] colored maps and manufacturing eternal cardboard necklaces[12]. He was inclined to drowse off to sleep[13] in the middle of these tasks, a habit which both irritated and frightened his young teacher. To his relief[14] she complained to his parents, and he was removed from the school. The Roger Buttons told their friends that they felt he was too young.

1 **at ease:** à vontade • 2 **somewhat in awe of him:** um pouco intimidados por ele • 3 **puzzled:** perplexo • 4 **he read up on it in the medical journal:** ele pesquisou publicações médicas • 5 **urging:** insistência • 6 **the milder games:** jogos mais leves • 7 **football:** futebol americano • 8 **to knit:** reconstituir-se • 9 **kindergarten:** jardim de infância • 10 **pasting:** colar • 11 **weaving:** elaborar; criar • 12 **cardboard necklaces:** colares de cartolina • 13 **he was inclined to drowse off to sleep:** tinha o costume de cochilar • 14 **to his relief:** para seu alívio

By the time he was twelve years old his parents had grown used to him[1]. Indeed, so strong is the force of custom that they no longer[2] felt that he was different from any other child—except when some curious anomaly reminded them of the fact. But one day a few weeks after his twelfth birthday, while looking in the mirror, Benjamin made, or thought he made, an astonishing discovery. Did his eyes deceive[3] him, or had his hair turned in the dozen years of his life from white to iron-gray[4] under its concealing dye? Was the network of wrinkles[5] on his face becoming less pronounced? Was his skin healthier and firmer, with even a touch of ruddy[6] winter color? He could not tell. He knew that he no longer stooped[7], and that his physical condition had improved since the early days of his life.

"Can it be——?" he thought to himself, or, rather, scarcely dared to think[8].

He went to his father. "I am grown," he announced determinedly. "I want to put on long trousers."

His father hesitated. "Well," he said finally, "I don't know. Fourteen is the age for putting on long trousers—and you are only twelve."

"But you'll have to admit," protested Benjamin, "that I'm big for my age."

His father looked at him with illusory speculation. "Oh, I'm not so sure of that," he said. "I was as big as you when I was twelve."

1 **had grown used to him:** haviam se acostumado com ele • 2 **no longer:** já não • 3 **deceive:** enganavam • 4 **iron gray:** cinza metálico • 5 **network of wrinkles:** conjunto de rugas • 6 **ruddy:** saudável • 7 **stooped:** caminhava encurvado • 8 **scarcely dared to think:** quase não se atrevia a pensar

This was not true—it was all part of Roger Button's silent agreement with himself to believe in his son's normality.

Finally a compromise was reached. Benjamin was to continue to dye his hair. He was to make a better attempt to play with boys of his own age. He was not to wear his spectacles or carry a cane in the street. In return for these concessions he was allowed his first suit of long trousers. . . .

IV

Of the life of Benjamin Button between his twelfth and twenty-first year I intend to say little. Suffice to record that[1] they were years of normal ungrowth. When Benjamin was eighteen he was erect[2] as a man of fifty; he had more hair and it was of a dark gray; his step was firm[3], his voice had lost its cracked quaver and descended to a healthy baritone. So his father sent him up to Connecticut to take examinations for entrance to Yale College. Benjamin passed his examination and became a member of the freshman class[4].

On the third day following his matriculation he received a notification from Mr. Hart, the college registrar, to call at his office and arrange his schedule[5]. Benjamin, glancing[6] in the mirror, decided that his hair needed a new application of its brown dye, but an anxious inspection of his bureau[7]

1 **suffice to record that:** basta lembrar que • 2 **erect:** ereto • 3 **his step was firm:** seu passo era firme • 4 **freshman class:** turma dos calouros • 5 **schedule:** horário • 6 **glancing:** lançando um olhar rápido • 7 **bureau:** escrivaninha

drawer disclosed that the dye bottle was not there. Then he remembered—he had emptied it the day before and thrown it away.

He was in a dilemma. He was due at the registrar's in five minutes[1]. There seemed to be no help for it—he must go as he was. He did.

"Good-morning," said the registrar politely. "You've come to inquire about your son."

"Why[2], as a matter of fact, my name's Button—" began Benjamin, but Mr. Hart cut him off[3].

"I'm very glad to meet you, Mr. Button. I'm expecting your son here any minute."

"That's me!" burst out[4] Benjamin. "I'm a freshman[5]."

"What!"

"I'm a freshman."

"Surely you're joking."

"Not at all."

The registrar frowned and glanced at a card before[6] him. "Why, I have Mr. Benjamin Button's age down here as eighteen."

"That's my age," asserted Benjamin, flushing slightly[7].

The registrar eyed him wearily[8]. "Now surely, Mr. Button, you don't expect me to believe that."

Benjamin smiled wearily. "I am eighteen," he repeated.

The registrar pointed sternly to the door. "Get out," he

1 **he was due at the registrar's in five minutes:** tinha uma reunião com o responsável pelas matrículas dentro de cinco minutos • 2 **why:** bem • 3 **cut him off:** cortou-o; interrompeu-o • 4 **burst out:** explodiu • 5 **freshman:** calouro • 6 **before:** diante • 7 **flushing slightly:** enrubescendo um pouco • 8 **eyed him wearily:** lançou um olhar cansado

said. "Get out of college[1] and get out of town. You are a dangerous lunatic."

"I am eighteen."

Mr. Hart opened the door. "The idea!" he shouted. "A man of your age trying to enter here as a freshman. Eighteen years old, are you? Well, I'll give you eighteen minutes to get out of town."

Benjamin Button walked with dignity from the room, and half a dozen undergraduates[2], who were waiting in the hall, followed him curiously with their eyes. When he had gone a little way he turned around[3], faced the infuriated[4] registrar, who was still standing in the doorway, and repeated in a firm voice: "I am eighteen years old."

To a chorus of titters which went up from[5] the group of undergraduates, Benjamin walked away.

But he was not fated to[6] escape so easily. On his melancholy walk to the railroad station he found that he was being followed by a group, then by a swarm[7], and finally by a dense mass of undergraduates. The word had gone around that a lunatic had passed the entrance examinations for Yale and attempted to palm himself off as a youth of eighteen. A fever of excitement permeated the college. Men ran hatless[8] out of classes, the football team abandoned its practice and joined the mob[9], professors' wives with bonnets awry and bustles

1 **college:** universidade • 2 **undergraduates:** estudantes universitários que ainda não se formaram • 3 **he turned around:** se voltou • 4 **infuriated:** furioso • 5 **to a chorus of titters which went up from:** o som de um coro de risadas dissimuladas que vinham de • 6 **he was not fated to:** não estava fadado • 7 **swarm:** enxame, multidão • 8 **hatless:** sem chapéu (algo inusitado para a época) • 9 **mob:** multidão

out of position[1], ran shouting after the procession, from which proceeded a continual succession of remarks aimed at[2] the tender sensibilities[3] of Benjamin Button.

"He must be the Wandering Jew[4]!"

"He ought to go to prep school[5] at his age!"

"Look at the infant prodigy!"

"He thought this was the old men's home[6]."

"Go up to Harvard!"

Benjamin increased his gait[7], and soon he was running. He would show them! He *would* go to Harvard, and then they would regret these ill-considered taunts[8]!

Safely on board[9] the train for Baltimore, he put his head from the window. "You'll regret this!" he shouted.

"Ha-ha!" the undergraduates laughed. "Ha-ha-ha!" It was the biggest mistake that Yale College had ever made. . . .

V

In 1880 Benjamin Button was twenty years old, and he signalized his birthday by going to work for his father in Roger Button & Co., Wholesale Hardware. It was in that same year

1 **professors' wives with bonnets awry and bustles out of position:** as esposas dos catedráticos com os chapéus tortos e as anquinhas fora de lugar (anquinhas eram armações de arame usadas sob o vestido para dar maior volume às saias) • 2 **aimed at:** dirigidos a • 3 **tender sensibilities:** sensíveis suscetibilidades • 4 **Wandering Jew:** judeu errante (personagem bíblico que se negou a dar água a Jesus, que o condenou a vagar pelo mundo até o fim dos tempos) • 5 **prep school (preparatory school):** escola secundária que prepara alunos para entrar na universidade • 6 **old men's home:** asilo para homens • 7 **gait:** passo • 8 **ill-considered taunts:** provocações maliciosas • 9 **on board:** a bordo

that he began "going out socially"—that is, his father insisted on taking him to several fashionable dances. Roger Button was now fifty, and he and his son were more and more companionable[1]—in fact, since Benjamin had ceased to dye his hair (which was still grayish) they appeared about the same age, and could have passed for brothers.

One night in August they got into the phaeton attired in their full-dress suits and drove out to a dance at the Shevlins' country house, situated just outside of Baltimore. It was a gorgeous[2] evening. A full moon drenched[3] the road to the lusterless[4] color of platinum, and late-blooming harvest flowers[5] breathed into the motionless air aromas that were like low, half-heard laughter[6]. The open country, carpeted for rods around with bright wheat[7], was translucent as in the day. It was almost impossible not to be affected by the sheer[8] beauty of the sky—almost.

"There's a great future in the dry-goods business[9]," Roger Button was saying. He was not a spiritual man—his aesthetic sense was rudimentary.

"Old fellows like me can't learn new tricks[10]," he observed profoundly. "It's you youngsters with energy and vitality that have the great future before you."

Far up the road the lights of the Shevlins' country house

1 **companionable:** amigáveis • 2 **gorgeous:** maravilhosa • 3 **drenched:** inundava • 4 **lusterless:** opaca • 5 **late-blooming harvest flowers:** as últimas flores da estação • 6 **laughter:** risada • 7 **carpeted for rods around with bright wheat:** coberto ao longo de muitos metros com hastes de trigo brilhantes • 8 **sheer:** absoluta • 9 **the dry-goods business:** indústria têxtil • 10 **tricks:** habilidades

drifted into view[1], and presently there was a sighing sound[2] that crept[3] persistently toward them—it might have been the fine plaint[4] of violins or the rustle[5] of the silver wheat under the moon.

They pulled up[6] behind a handsome brougham[7] whose passengers were disembarking at the door. A lady got out, then an elderly[8] gentleman, then another young lady, beautiful as sin[9]. Benjamin started[10]; an almost chemical change seemed to dissolve and recompose the very elements of his body. A rigor passed over him, blood rose into his cheeks[11], his forehead, and there was a steady thumping[12] in his ears. It was first love.

The girl was slender and frail[13], with hair that was ashen[14] under the moon and honey-colored under the sputtering[15] gas-lamps of the porch. Over her shoulders was thrown a Spanish mantilla of softest yellow, butterflied in black[16]; her feet were glittering buttons at the hem of her bustled dress[17].

Roger Button leaned over[18] to his son. "That," he said, "is young Hildegarde Moncrief, the daughter of General Moncrief."

Benjamin nodded[19] coldly. "Pretty little thing," he said

1 **drifted into view:** ia se vislumbrando pouco a pouco • 2 **a sighing sound:** um som como um suspiro • 3 **crept:** se arrastava • 4 **plaint:** pranto • 5 **rustle:** sussurro • 6 **they pulled up:** pararam • 7 **brougham:** tipo de carruagem • 8 **elderly:** de idade avançada • 9 **beautiful as sin:** bela como o pecado • 10 **started:** sobressaltou-se • 11 **cheeks:** maçãs do rosto • 12 **a steady thumping:** uma pancada constante • 13 **slender and frail:** delgada e delicada • 14 **ashen:** de cor cinza • 15 **sputtering:** faiscante • 16 **butterflied in black:** com detalhes praticamente em formato de borboletas pretas • 17 **glittering buttons at the hem of her bustled dress:** botões brilhantes na bainha de seu vestido com anquinhas • 18 **leaned over:** se inclinou na direção de • 19 **nodded:** assentiu

indifferently. But when the Negro boy had led the buggy[1] away, he added: "Dad, you might introduce me to her."

They approached a group, of which Miss Moncrief was the center. Reared in the old tradition[2], she courtesied[3] low before Benjamin. Yes, he might have a dance. He thanked her and walked away—staggered away[4].

The interval until the time for his turn should arrive dragged itself out interminably[5]. He stood close to the wall, silent, inscrutable, watching with murderous[6] eyes the young bloods[7] of Baltimore as they eddied around[8] Hildegarde Moncrief, passionate admiration in their faces. How obnoxious[9] they seemed to Benjamin; how intolerably rosy[10]! Their curling brown whiskers[11] aroused in him a feeling equivalent to indigestion.

But when his own time came, and he drifted with her out[12] upon the changing floor to the music of the latest waltz from Paris, his jealousies and anxieties melted[13] from him like a mantle of snow. Blind with enchantment, he felt that life was just beginning.

"You and your brother got here just as we did, didn't you?" asked Hildegarde, looking up at him with eyes that were like bright blue enamel[14].

1 **buggy:** caleça • 2 **reared in the old tradition:** criada na velha tradição • 3 **she courtesied:** fez uma reverência • 4 **staggered away:** cambaleando • 5 **dragged itself out interminably:** se arrastou infinitamente • 6 **murderous:** assassinos • 7 **the young bloods:** os jovens de boa família • 8 **they eddied around:** eles se aglomeravam em volta de • 9 **obnoxious:** repugnantes • 10 **rosy:** otimistas • 11 **whiskers:** bigodes • 12 **he drifted with her out:** saiu com ela • 13 **melted:** se derreteram • 14 **enamel:** esmalte

Benjamin hesitated. If she took him for his father's brother, would it be best to enlighten her[1]? He remembered his experience at Yale, so he decided against it[2]. It would be rude to contradict a lady; it would be criminal to mar[3] this exquisite occasion with the grotesque story of his origin. Later, perhaps. So he nodded, smiled, listened, was happy.

"I like men of your age," Hildegarde told him. "Young boys are so idiotic. They tell me how much champagne they drink at college, and how much money they lose playing cards. Men of your age know how to appreciate women."

Benjamin felt himself on the verge of[4] a proposal—with an effort he choked back the impulse[5].

"You're just the romantic age," she continued—"fifty. Twenty-five is too wordly-wise[6]; thirty is apt to be pale from overwork[7]; forty is the age of long stories that take a whole cigar to tell; sixty is—oh, sixty is too near seventy; but fifty is the mellow[8] age. I love fifty."

Fifty seemed to Benjamin a glorious age. He longed[9] passionately to be fifty.

"I've always said," went on Hildegarde, "that I'd rather marry a man of fifty and be taken care of than many a man of thirty and take care of *him*."

For Benjamin the rest of the evening was bathed in a hon-

1 **to enlighten her:** esclarecê-la • 2 **he decided against it:** decidiu não fazer isso • 3 **to mar:** arruinar • 4 **on the verge of:** a ponto de • 5 **he choked back the impulse:** reprimiu o impulso • 6 **worldly-wise:** mundano • 7 **is apt to be pale from overwork:** tendem a estar abatidos pela sobrecarga de trabalho • 8 **mellow:** madura; tranquila • 9 **he longed:** desejava

ey-colored mist[1]. Hildegarde gave him two more dances, and they discovered that they were marvelously in accord[2] on all the questions of the day[3]. She was to go driving with him on the following Sunday, and then they would discuss all these questions further.

Going home in the phaeton just before the crack of dawn[4], when the first bees were humming[5] and the fading moon glimmered in the cool dew[6], Benjamin knew vaguely that his father was discussing wholesale hardware.

"....And what do you think should merit our biggest attention after hammers and nails[7]?" the elder Button was saying.

"Love," replied Benjamin absent-mindedly[8].

"Lugs[9]?" exclaimed Roger Button, "Why, I've just covered the question of lugs."

Benjamin regarded him with dazed eyes[10] just as the eastern sky was suddenly cracked with light, and an oriole yawned piercingly in the quickening trees[11]....

VI

When, six months later, the engagement of Miss Hilde-

1 **bathed in a honey-colored mist:** banhada numa neblina cor de mel • 2 **in accord:** de acordo • 3 **the questions of the day:** os temas da atualidade • 4 **the crack of dawn:** o despontar do dia • 5 **the first bees were humming:** as primeiras abelhas zuniam • 6 **the fading moon glimmered in the cool dew:** a lua que desaparecia brilhava no orvalho fresco • 7 **hammers and nails:** martelos e pregos • 8 **absent-mindedly:** distraidamente • 9 **lugs:** suportes de madeira • 10 **with dazed eyes:** com olhos aturdidos; atônitos • 11 **an oriole yawned piercingly in the quickening trees:** um papa-figo os observava fixamente das árvores da estrada enquanto passavam

garde Moncrief to Mr. Benjamin Button was made known (I say "made known," for General Moncrief declared he would rather fall upon his sword[1] than announce it), the excitement in Baltimore society reached a feverish pitch[2]. The almost forgotten story of Benjamin's birth was remembered and sent out upon the winds of scandal[3] in picaresque and incredible forms. It was said that Benjamin was really the father of Roger Button, that he was his brother who had been in prison for forty years, that he was John Wilkes Booth[4] in disguise[5]—and, finally, that he had two small conical horns[6] sprouting[7] from his head.

The Sunday supplements of the New York papers played up[8] the case with fascinating sketches which showed the head of Benjamin Button attached to a fish, to a snake, and, finally, to a body of solid brass[9]. He became known, journalistically, as the Mystery Man of Maryland. But the true story, as is usually the case, had a very small circulation.

However, every one agreed with General Moncrief that it was "criminal" for a lovely girl who could have married any beau[10] in Baltimore to throw herself into the arms of a man who was assuredly[11] fifty. In vain Mr. Roger Button published his son's birth certificate in large type[12] in the Baltimore *Blaze*. No one believed it. You had only to look at Benjamin and see.

1 **he would rather fall upon his sword:** preferia se matar • 2 **reached a feverish pitch:** chegou a um ponto extremo • 3 **sent out upon the winds of scandal:** foi aumentada com os rumores do escândalo • 4 **John Wilkes Booth:** o assassino de Abraham Lincoln • 5 **in disguise:** disfarçado • 6 **conical horns:** chifres em forma de cone • 7 **sprouting:** saindo • 8 **played up:** exageraram • 9 **brass:** latão • 10 **any beau:** qualquer galã • 11 **assuredly:** sem dúvida • 12 **in large type:** em letras grandes

On the part of the two people most concerned there was no wavering[1]. So many of the stories about her fiancé[2] were false that Hildegarde refused stubbornly[3] to believe even the true one. In vain General Moncrief pointed out to her the high mortality among men of fifty—or, at least, among men who looked fifty; in vain he told her of the instability of the wholesale hardware business. Hildegarde had chosen to marry for mellowness[4], and marry she did. . . .

VII

In one particular, at least, the friends of Hildegarde Moncrief were mistaken. The wholesale hardware business prospered amazingly. In the fifteen years between Benjamin Button's marriage in 1880 and his father's retirement in 1895, the family fortune was doubled—and this was due largely to the younger member of the firm.

Needless to say[5], Baltimore eventually[6] received the couple to its bosom[7]. Even old General Moncrief became reconciled to his son-in-law[8] when Benjamin gave him the money to bring out[9] his "History of the Civil War" in twenty volumes, which had been refused by nine prominent publishers.

In Benjamin himself fifteen years had wrought[10] many changes. It seemed to him that the blood flowed with new

1 **there was no wavering:** não havia dúvida • 2 **fiancé:** noivo • 3 **stubbornly:** obstinadamente • 4 **mellowness:** maturidade • 5 **needless to say:** desnecessário dizer • 6 **eventually:** finalmente • 7 **received the couple to its bosom:** acolheu o casal em seu seio • 8 **son-in-law:** genro • 9 **bring out:** publicar • 10 **had wrought:** haviam provocado

vigor through his veins[1]. It began to be a pleasure to rise in the morning, to walk with an active step along the busy, sunny street, to work untiringly[2] with his shipments of hammers and his cargoes[3] of nails. It was in 1890 that he executed his famous business coup[4]: he brought up the suggestion[5] that *all nails used in nailing up the boxes*[6] *in which nails are shipped are the property of the shippee*[7], a proposal which became a statute, was approved by Chief Justice[8] Fossile, and saved Roger Button and Company, Wholesale Hardware, more than *six hundred nails every year.*

In addition, Benjamin discovered that he was becoming more and more attracted by the gay side of life[9]. It was typical of his growing enthusiasm for pleasure that he was the first man in the city of Baltimore to own[10] and run an automobile. Meeting him on the street, his contemporaries would stare enviously at the picture he made of health and vitality.

"He seems to grow younger every year," they would remark. And if old Roger Button, now sixty-five years old, had failed at first to give a proper welcome to his son he atoned[11] at last by bestowing on him what amounted to adulation[12].

1 **flowed with new vigor through his veins:** corria com novo vigor em suas veias • 2 **untiringly:** incansavelmente • 3 **cargoes:** cargas • 4 **business coup:** golpe mestre nos negócios • 5 **he brought up the suggestion:** sugeriu • 6 **all nails used in nailing up the boxes:** todos os pregos usados para fechar as caixas • 7 **shippee:** remetente • 8 **Chief Justice:** presidente do tribunal • 9 **the gay side of life:** o lado alegre da vida • 10 **to own:** possuir • 11 **he atoned:** o compensou • 12 **by bestowing on him what amounted to adulation:** concedendo-lhe o que beirava a adulação

And here we come to an unpleasant subject which it will be well to pass over[1] as quickly as possible. There was only one thing that worried Benjamin Button; his wife had ceased to attract him.

At that time Hildegarde was a woman of thirty-five, with a son, Roscoe, fourteen years old. In the early days of their marriage Benjamin had worshipped her[2]. But, as the years passed, her honey-colored hair became an unexciting brown, the blue enamel of her eyes assumed the aspect of cheap crockery[3]—moreover, and, most of all, she had become too settled in her ways[4], too placid, too content[5], too anemic[6] in her excitements, and too sober[7] in her taste. As a bride[8] it had been she who had "dragged[9]" Benjamin to dances and dinners—now conditions were reversed. She went out socially with him, but without enthusiasm, devoured already by that eternal inertia which comes to live with each of us one day and stays with us to the end.

Benjamin's discontent waxed stronger[10]. At the outbreak of the Spanish-American War in 1898 his home had for him so little charm that he decided to join the army. With his business influence he obtained a commission[11] as captain, and proved so adaptable to the work that he was made a major[12], and finally a lieutenant-colonel[13] just in time to participate

1 **to pass over:** passar por cima • 2 **had worshipped her:** a idolatrava • 3 **cheap crockery:** cerâmica barata • 4 **too settled in her ways:** demasiado acomodada em suas maneiras • 5 **content:** conformista • 6 **anemic:** falta de energia • 7 **sober:** comedida • 8 **bride:** noiva • 9 **had dragged:** havia arrastado • 10 **waxed stronger:** foi aumentando cada vez mais • 11 **commission:** patente • 12 **major:** comandante • 13 **lieutenant-colonel:** tenente-coronel

in the celebrated charge[1] up San Juan Hill[2]. He was slightly wounded[3], and received a medal.

Benjamin had become so attached to the activity and excitement of army life[4] that he regretted to give it up[5], but his business required attention, so he resigned his commission[6] and came home. He was met at the station by a brass band[7] and escorted to his house.

VIII

Hildegarde, waving a large silk flag[8], greeted him on the porch, and even as he kissed her he felt with a sinking of the heart[9] that these three years had taken their toll[10]. She was a woman of forty now, with a faint skirmish line of gray hairs[11] in her head. The sight depressed him.

Up in his room he saw his reflection in the familiar mirror—he went closer and examined his own face with anxiety, comparing it after a moment with a photograph of himself in uniform taken just before the war.

"Good Lord!" he said aloud. The process was continu-

1 **charge:** tomada • 2 **San Juan Hill:** Colina de San Juan (onde ocorreu em 1898 a batalha mais famosa da guerra hispano-americana)• 3 **he was slightly wounded:** foi levemente ferido • 4 **army life:** vida militar • 5 **he regretted to give it up:** lamentava ter de deixá-la • 6 **he resigned his commission:** renunciou ao seu cargo • 7 **a brass band:** banda de metais • 8 **waving a large silk flag:** acenando com uma grande bandeira de seda • 9 **a sinking of the heart:** com o coração oprimido • 10 **these three years had taken their toll:** aqueles três anos haviam deixado sua marca • 11 **a faint skirmish line of gray hairs:** uma tênue linha de cabelos grisalhos

ing. There was no doubt of it—he looked now like a man of thirty. Instead of being delighted[1], he was uneasy[2]—he was growing younger. He had hitherto[3] hoped that once he reached a bodily[4] age equivalent to his age in years, the grotesque phenomenon which had marked his birth would cease to function. He shuddered[5]. His destiny seemed to him awful[6], incredible.

When he came downstairs Hildegarde was waiting for him. She appeared annoyed, and he wondered if she had at last discovered that there was something amiss[7]. It was with an effort to relieve the tension between them that he broached the matter[8] at dinner in what he considered a delicate way.

"Well," he remarked lightly, "everybody says I look younger than ever."

Hildegarde regarded him with scorn[9]. She sniffed[10]. "Do you think it's anything to boast about[11]?"

"I'm not boasting," he asserted uncomfortably.

She sniffed again. "The idea," she said, and after a moment: "I should think you'd have enough pride to stop it."

"How can I?" he demanded.

"I'm not going to argue with you," she retorted[12]. "But there's a right way of doing things and a wrong way. If you've

1 **delighted:** encantado • 2 **uneasy:** pouco à vontade • 3 **hitherto:** até aquele momento • 4 **a bodily age:** uma idade corporal • 5 **he shuddered:** ele estremeceu • 6 **his destiny seemed to him awful:** seu destino lhe parecia terrível • 7 **there was something amiss:** algo estava errado • 8 **he broached the matter:** abordou o tema • 9 **scorn:** desdém • 10 **she sniffed:** disse com desdém • 11 **to boast about:** para se vangloriar • 12 **she retorted:** replicou

made up your mind to be different from everybody else, I don't suppose I can stop you, but I really don't think it's very considerate."

"But, Hildegarde, I can't help it[1]."

"You can too[2]. You're simply stubborn[3]. You think you don't want to be like any one else. You always have been that way, and you always will be. But just think how it would be if every one else looked at things as you do—what would the world be like?"

As this was an inane[4] and unanswerable argument Benjamin made no reply, and from that time on a chasm began to widen between them[5]. He wondered what possible fascination she had ever exercised over him.

To add to the breach[6], he found, as the new century gathered headway[7], that his thirst for gaiety[8] grew stronger. Never a party of any kind in the city of Baltimore but he was there[9], dancing with the prettiest of the young married women, chatting[10] with the most popular of the débutantes, and finding their company charming, while his wife, a dowager of evil omen[11], sat among the chaperons[12], now in haughty disapproval[13], and now following him with solemn, puzzled, and reproachful[14] eyes.

1 **I can't help it:** não posso evitar isso • 2 **you can too:** você pode, sim • 3 **stubborn:** teimoso • 4 **inane:** tola • 5 **a chasm began to widen between them:** começou a se abrir um abismo entre eles • 6 **to add to the breach:** para aumentar o abismo • 7 **as the new century gathered headway:** à medida que o novo século avançava • 8 **his thirst for gaiety:** sua sede de diversão • 9 **never a party ... but (that) he was there:** não havia festa em que ele não estivesse • 10 **chatting:** conversando • 11 **a dowager of evil omen:** uma viúva de mau agouro • 12 **chaperons:** acompanhantes • 13 **in haughty disapproval:** com um olhar altivo de desaprovação • 14 **reproachful:** reprovadores

"Look!" people would remark. "What a pity[1]! A young fellow that age tied to a woman of forty-five. He must be twenty years younger than his wife." They had forgotten—as people inevitably forget—that back in 1880 their mammas and papas had also remarked about this same ill-matched pair[2].

Benjamin's growing unhappiness at home was compensated for by his many new interests. He took up golf[3] and made a great success of it. He went in for dancing[4]: in 1906 he was an expert at "The Boston[5]," and in 1908 he was considered proficient at the "Maxixe[6]," while in 1909 his "Castle Walk[7]" was the envy of every young man in town.

His social activities, of course, interfered to some extent with his business, but then he had worked hard at wholesale hardware for twenty-five years and felt that he could soon hand it on to his son[8], Roscoe, who had recently graduated from Harvard.

He and his son were, in fact, often mistaken for each other. This pleased Benjamin—he soon forgot the insidious fear which had come over him on his return from the Spanish-American War, and grew to take a naïve pleasure in his appearance. There was only one fly in the delicious ointment[9]—he hated to appear in public with his wife. Hildegarde was almost fifty, and the sight of her made him feel absurd. . . .

1 **what a pity:** que pena • 2 **ill-matched pair:** casal que não combinava • 3 **he took up golf:** começou a jogar golfe • 4 **he went in for dancing:** saía para dançar • 5 **The Boston:** o nome original da valsa americana • 6 **Maxixe:** dança da época • 7 **Castle walk:** dança da época semelhante ao tango • 8 **hand it on to his son:** deixá-lo nas mãos de seu filho • 9 **one fly in the delicious ointment:** um problema

IX

One September day in 1910—a few years after Roger Button & Co., Wholesale Hardware, had been handed over to young Roscoe Button—a man, apparently about twenty years old, entered himself as a freshman at Harvard University in Cambridge. He did not make the mistake of announcing that he would never see fifty again nor did he mention the fact that his son had been graduated from the same institution ten years before.

He was admitted, and almost immediately attained a prominent position in the class, partly because he seemed a little older than the other freshmen, whose average age was about eighteen.

But his success was largely due to the fact that in the football game with Yale he played so brilliantly, with so much dash[1] and with such a cold, remorseless anger[2] that he scored seven touchdowns[3] and fourteen field goals[4] for Harvard, and caused one entire eleven of Yale men to be carried singly[5] from the field, unconscious. He was the most celebrated man in college.

Strange to say[6], in his third or junior year he was scarcely able to "make" the team[7]. The coaches said that he had lost weight, and it seemed to the more observant among them

1 **dash:** brio • 2 **remorseless anger:** ira implacável • 3 **touchdown:** a forma mais comum de marcar pontos no futebol americano: consiste em pegar a bola na zona de pontuação do adversário ou em cruzar a linha de gol de posse da bola • 4 **field goal:** quando se obtêm pontos (três) com um chute • 5 **singly:** um por um • 6 **strange to say:** por estranho que pareça • 7 **to "make" the team:** entrar no time

that he was not quite as tall as before. He made no touchdowns—indeed[1], he was retained on the team chiefly in hope that his enormous reputation would bring terror and disorganization to the Yale team.

In his senior year he did not make the team at all. He had grown so slight and frail[2] that one day he was taken by some sophomores[3] for a freshman, an incident which humiliated him terribly. He became known as something of a prodigy—a senior who was surely no more than sixteen—and he was often shocked at the worldliness[4] of some of his classmates. His studies seemed harder to him—he felt that they were too advanced. He had heard his classmates speak of St. Midas', the famous preparatory school, at which so many of them had prepared for college, and he determined after his graduation to enter himself at St. Midas', where the sheltered life[5] among boys his own size would be more congenial[6] to him.

Upon his graduation in 1914 he went home to Baltimore with his Harvard diploma in his pocket. Hildegarde was now residing in Italy, so Benjamin went to live with his son, Roscoe. But though he was welcomed in a general way, there was obviously no heartiness[7] in Roscoe's feeling toward him—there was even perceptible a tendency on his son's part to think that Benjamin, as he moped about the house[8] in adolescent mooniness[9], was somewhat in the way[10].

1 **indeed:** na verdade • 2 **frail:** frágil • 3 **sophomores:** estudantes do segundo ano da faculdade • 4 **shocked at the worldliness:** chocado com a superficialidade • 5 **the sheltered life:** a vida protegida • 6 **congenial:** agradável • 7 **heartiness:** sinceridade • 8 **as he moped about the house:** quando andava deprimido pela casa • 9 **in adolescent mooniness:** distraído como um adolescente • 10 **in the way:** um incômodo

Roscoe was married now and prominent in Baltimore life, and he wanted no scandal to creep out[1] in connection with his family.

Benjamin, no longer persona grata with the débutantes and younger college set[2], found himself left much alone[3], except for the companionship of three or four fifteen-year-old boys in the neighborhood. His idea of going to St. Midas' school recurred to him[4].

"Say," he said to Roscoe one day, "I've told you over and over[5] that I want to go to prep school."

"Well, go, then," replied Roscoe shortly. The matter was distasteful[6] to him, and he wished to avoid a discussion.

"I can't go alone," said Benjamin helplessly. "You'll have to enter me and take me up there."

"I haven't got time," declared Roscoe abruptly. His eyes narrowed[7] and he looked uneasily[8] at his father. "As a matter of fact," he added, "you'd better not go on with this business[9] much longer. You better pull up short[10]. You better—you better"—he paused and his face crimsoned as he sought for words[11]—"you better turn right around and start back the other way. This has gone too far to be a joke. It isn't funny any longer. You—you behave yourself!"

1 **to creep out:** que ocorresse • 2 **younger college set:** o círculo de jovens universitários • 3 **found himself left much alone:** se sentia muito só • 4 **recurred to him:** voltava-lhe à mente • 5 **over and over:** várias vezes • 6 **distasteful:** desagradável • 7 **narrowed:** se estreitaram • 8 **uneasily:** com rancor • 9 **you'd better not go on with this business:** melhor parar com este negócio • 10 **you better pull up short:** melhor parar já • 11 **his face crimsoned as he sought for words:** seu rosto ficou vermelho enquanto ele buscava as palavras

Benjamin looked at him, on the verge of tears[1].

"And another thing," continued Roscoe, "when visitors are in the house I want you to call me 'Uncle'—not 'Roscoe,' but 'Uncle,' do you understand? It looks absurd for a boy of fifteen to call me by my first name. Perhaps you'd better call me 'Uncle' *all* the time, so you'll get used to it."

With a harsh look[2] at his father, Roscoe turned away....

X

At the termination of this interview, Benjamin wandered dismally[3] upstairs and stared at himself in the mirror. He had not shaved for three months, but he could find nothing on his face but a faint white down[4] with which it seemed unnecessary to meddle[5]. When he had first come home from Harvard, Roscoe had approached him with the proposition that he should wear eye-glasses and imitation whiskers glued[6] to his cheeks, and it had seemed for a moment that the farce[7] of his early years was to be repeated. But whiskers had itched[8] and made him ashamed[9]. He wept and Roscoe had reluctantly relented[10].

Benjamin opened a book of boys' stories, "The Boy Scouts in Bimini Bay," and began to read. But he found him-

1 **on the verge of tears:** à beira das lágrimas • 2 **a harsh look:** um olhar duro • 3 **wandered dismally:** subiu tristemente • 4 **down:** penugem • 5 **to meddle:** interferir • 6 **glued:** colado • 7 **farce:** farsa • 8 **had itched:** havia coçado (o bigode falso) • 9 **ashamed:** envergonhado • 10 **had reluctantly relented:** cedeu com relutância

self thinking persistently about the war. America had joined the Allied[1] cause during the preceding month, and Benjamin wanted to enlist, but, alas[2], sixteen was the minimum age, and he did not look that old. His true age, which was fifty-seven, would have disqualified him[3], anyway.

There was a knock at his door, and the butler[4] appeared with a letter bearing[5] a large official legend in the corner and addressed to Mr. Benjamin Button. Benjamin tore it open eagerly[6], and read the enclosure[7] with delight. It informed him that many reserve officers who had served in the Spanish-American War were being called back into service with a higher rank[8], and it enclosed his commission as brigadier-general in the United States army with orders to report[9] immediately.

Benjamin jumped to his feet fairly quivering[10] with enthusiasm. This was what he had wanted. He seized his cap[11] and ten minutes later he had entered a large tailoring establishment on Charles Street, and asked in his uncertain treble[12] to be measured for a uniform.

"Want to play soldier, sonny[13]?" demanded a clerk casually.

Benjamin flushed. "Say[14]! Never mind what I want!" he retorted angrily. "My name's Button and I live on Mt. Ver-

1 **Allied:** Aliados (da Primeira Guerra Mundial) • 2 **alas:** infelizmente • 3 **would have disqualified him:** o que o teria desqualificado • 4 **butler:** mordomo • 5 **bearing:** na qual havia • 6 **tore it open eagerly:** abriu com entusiasmo • 7 **enclosure:** documento incluso • 8 **rank:** patente • 9 **to report:** se apresentar • 10 **fairly quivering:** tremendo ostensivamente • 11 **he seized his cap:** pegou seu quepe • 12 **treble:** voz esganiçada • 13 **sonny:** garoto • 14 **say:** escute

non Place, so you know I'm good for it[1]."

"Well," admitted the clerk hesitantly, "if you're not, I guess your daddy[2] is, all right."

Benjamin was measured, and a week later his uniform was completed. He had difficulty in obtaining the proper[3] general's insignia because the dealer kept insisting to Benjamin that a nice Y. W. C. A.[4] badge[5] would look just as well and be much more fun to play with.

Saying nothing to Roscoe, he left the house one night and proceeded by train to Camp Mosby, in South Carolina, where he was to command an infantry brigade. On a sultry[6] April day he approached the entrance to the camp, paid off the taxicab[7] which had brought him from the station, and turned to the sentry[8] on guard.

"Get some one to handle my luggage!" he said briskly[9].

The sentry eyed him reproachfully. "Say," he remarked, "where you goin' with the general's duds[10], sonny?"

Benjamin, veteran of the Spanish-American War, whirled upon him[11] with fire in his eye, but with, alas, a changing treble voice.

"Come to attention!" he tried to thunder[12]; he paused for breath—then suddenly he saw the sentry snap his heels together[13] and bring his rifle to the present. Benjamin con-

1 **I'm good for it:** eu estou qualificado • 2 **daddy:** pai • 3 **proper:** adequada • 4 **Y.W.C.A. (Young Womens' Christian Association):** Associação Cristã de Moças • 5 **badge:** insígnia • 6 **sultry:** abafado • 7 **paid off the taxicab:** pagou o táxi • 8 **sentry:** sentinela • 9 **briskly:** rapidamente • 10 **duds:** farda • 11 **whirled upon him:** voltou-se para ele • 12 **to thunder:** gritou; esbravejou • 13 **snap his heels together:** juntou os joelhos no estilo militar

cealed a smile of gratification, but when he glanced around[1] his smile faded. It was not he who had inspired obedience, but an imposing artillery colonel who was approaching on horseback[2].

"Colonel!" called Benjamin shrilly[3].

The colonel came up, drew rein[4], and looked coolly down at him with a twinkle in his eyes[5]. "Whose little boy are you?" he demanded kindly.

"I'll soon darn[6] well show you whose little boy I am!" retorted Benjamin in a ferocious voice. "Get down off that horse!"

The colonel roared with laughter.

"You want him, eh, general?"

"Here!" cried Benjamin desperately. "Read this." And he thrust[7] his commission toward the colonel.

The colonel read it, his eyes popping from their sockets[8].

"Where'd you get this?" he demanded, slipping the document into his own pocket.

"I got it from the Government, as you'll soon find out!"

"You come along with me," said the colonel with a peculiar look. "We'll go up to headquarters and talk this over[9]. Come along[10]."

The colonel turned and began walking his horse in the direction of headquarters. There was nothing for Benjamin

1 **he glanced around:** olhou ao redor • 2 **on horseback:** montado a cavalo • 3 **shrilly:** estridentemente • 4 **drew rein:** controlou o cavalo com as rédeas • 5 **with a twinkle in his eyes:** com um brilho nos olhos • 6 **darn:** eufemismo para *damn*, "maldito" • 7 **he thrust:** jogou • 8 **his eyes popping from their sockets:** os olhos saltando das órbitas • 9 **talk this over:** falar sobre isso • 10 **come along:** me acompanhe

to do but follow with as much dignity as possible—meanwhile promising himself a stern revenge[1].

But this revenge did not materialize. Two days later, however, his son Roscoe materialized from Baltimore, hot and cross from a hasty trip[2], and escorted the weeping[3] general, *sans*[4] uniform, back to his home.

XI

In 1920 Roscoe Button's first child was born. During the attendant festivities[5], however, no one thought it "the thing" to mention, that the little grubby[6] boy, apparently about ten years of age who played around the house with lead soldiers and a miniature circus, was the new baby's own grandfather.

No one disliked the little boy whose fresh, cheerful face was crossed with just a hint of sadness[7], but to Roscoe Button his presence was a source of torment. In the idiom[8] of his generation Roscoe did not consider the matter "efficient." It seemed to him that his father, in refusing to look sixty, had not behaved like a "red-blooded he-man[9]"—this was Roscoe's favorite expression—but in a curious and perverse manner. Indeed, to think about the matter for as much as

1 **a stern revenge:** uma vingança terrível • 2 **hot and cross from a hasty trip:** esfogueado e cansado da viagem repentina • 3 **weeping:** choroso • 4 ***sans*:** sem (forma antiga) • 5 **the attendant festivities:** as devidas celebrações • 6 **grubby:** sujo • 7 **a hint of sadness:** toque de tristeza • 8 **idiom:** gíria • 9 **red-blooded he-man:** um homem como Deus quer

a half an hour drove him to the edge of insanity[1]. Roscoe believed that "live wires[2]" should keep young, but carrying it out on such a scale was—was—was inefficient. And there Roscoe rested[3].

Five years later Roscoe's little boy had grown old enough to play childish games with little Benjamin under the supervision of the same nurse. Roscoe took them both to kindergarten on the same day, and Benjamin found that playing with little strips[4] of colored paper, making mats[5] and chains and curious and beautiful designs, was the most fascinating game in the world. Once he was bad and had to stand in the corner—then he cried—but for the most part there were gay hours in the cheerful[6] room, with the sunlight coming in the windows and Miss Bailey's kind hand resting for a moment now and then in his tousled hair[7].

Roscoe's son moved up into the first grade[8] after a year, but Benjamin stayed on in the kindergarten[9]. He was very happy. Sometimes when other tots[10] talked about what they would do when they grew up[11] a shadow would cross his little face as if in a dim[12], childish way he realized that those were things in which he was never to share.

The days flowed on[13] in monotonous content. He went back a third year to the kindergarten, but he was too little

1 **drove him to the edge of insanity:** o levava à beira da loucura • 2 **"live wires":** pessoas dinâmicas • 3 **and there Roscoe rested:** e Roscoe ficava ali • 4 **strips:** tiras • 5 **mats:** tapetes • 6 **cheerful:** alegre • 7 **tousled hair:** cabelo despenteado • 8 **moved up into the first grade:** passou para o primeiro ano • 9 **stayed on in kindergarten:** permaneceu no jardim de infância • 10 **tots:** bebês • 11 **when they grew up:** quando crescessem • 12 **dim:** confusa 13 **the days flowed on:** os dias iam passando

now to understand what the bright shining strips of paper were for. He cried because the other boys were bigger than he and he was afraid of them[1]. The teacher talked to him, but though he tried to understand he could not understand at all.

He was taken from the kindergarten. His nurse, Nana, in her starched gingham dress[2], became the center of his tiny world. On bright days they walked in the park; Nana would point at a great gray monster and say "elephant," and Benjamin would say it after her, and when he was being undressed for bed that night he would say it over and over aloud to her: "Elyphant, elyphant, elyphant." Sometimes Nana let him jump on the bed, which was fun, because if you sat down exactly right it would bounce you up on your feet again[3], and if you said "Ah" for a long time while you jumped you got a very pleasing broken vocal effect.

He loved to take a big cane[4] from the hatrack[5] and go around hitting chairs and tables with it and saying: "Fight, fight, fight." When there were people there the old ladies would cluck at him[6], which interested him, and the young ladies would try to kiss him, which he submitted to with mild boredom[7]. And when the long day was done at five o'clock he would go up-stairs with Nana and be fed on oatmeal[8] and nice soft mushy[9] foods with a spoon.

1 **he was afraid of them:** tinha medo deles • 2 **starched gingham dress:** vestido de algodão engomado • 3 **it would bounce you up on your feet again:** você quicava e levantava de novo • 4 **cane:** bengala • 5 **hatrack:** porta-chapéus • 6 **would cluck at him:** falavam com ele estalando a língua • 7 **which he submitted to with mild boredom:** a que se submetia um pouco aborrecido • 8 **oatmeal:** mingau de aveia • 9 **mushy:** com consistência cremosa

There were no troublesome memories in his childish sleep; no token[1] came to him of his brave days at college, of the glittering years when he flustered[2] the hearts of many girls. There were only the white, safe walls of his crib and Nana and a man who came to see him sometimes, and a great big orange ball that Nana pointed at just before his twilight[3] bed hour and called "sun." When the sun went his eyes were sleepy—there were no dreams, no dreams to haunt him[4].

The past—the wild charge at the head of his men up San Juan Hill; the first years of his marriage when he worked late into the summer dusk[5] down in the busy city for young Hildegarde whom he loved; the days before that when he sat smoking far into the night[6] in the gloomy[7] old Button house on Monroe Street with his grandfather—all these had faded like unsubstantial dreams from his mind as though they had never been.

He did not remember. He did not remember clearly whether the milk was warm or cool at his last feeding or how the days passed—there was only his crib and Nana's familiar presence. And then he remembered nothing. When he was hungry he cried—that was all. Through the noons[8] and nights he breathed and over him there were soft mumblings and murmurings[9] that he scarcely heard, and faintly differentiated smells, and light and darkness.

1 **token:** recordação • 2 **he flustered:** ele agitava • 3 **twilight:** crepúsculo • 4 **no dreams to haunt him:** sem sonhos o assombrando • 5 **dusk:** anoitecer • 6 **far into the night:** até altas horas da noite • 7 **gloomy:** sombria • 8 **noons:** tardes • 9 **mumblings and murmurings:** vozes que murmuravam e sussurravam

Then it was all dark, and his white crib and the dim faces that moved above him, and the warm sweet aroma of the milk, faded out altogether from his mind.

John
Cheever

The Swimmer

"It was suddenly growing dark; it was that moment when the pin-headed birds seem to organize their song into some acute and knowledgeable recognition of the storm's approach."

BIOGRAFIA

John Cheever

Se não tivesse sido expulso da escola, "talvez tivesse sido empregado num posto de gasolina ou algo assim", disse em certa ocasião. Considerado o Tchékhov dos subúrbios, John Cheever (Quincy, Massachusetts, 1912 – Ossining, Nova York, 1982) trocou seus cadernos por uma máquina de escrever no dia em que o expulsaram da escola por fumar. Tinha 17 anos e precisou somente de alguns dias para completar sua primeira obra-prima, o conto "Expelled". Quando terminou, colocou-o num envelope e o enviou para *The New Republic*. Malcolm Cowley, editor da revista, o recebeu com certo ceticismo. "Nunca tínhamos publicado um conto de alguém tão jovem", disse, mas por fim o bom senso se impôs. O conto era um brilhante exercício de destruição de uma sociedade frívola baseada num sistema educacional "estúpido", ideia que J. D. Salinger (dez anos depois, na década de 1940) retomaria e elevaria à categoria de clássico em *O apanhador no campo de centeio*.

Cheever publicou, assim, seu primeiro conto em 1930 e se tornou aos 21 anos em colaborador habitual da revista *The New Yorker*. Tentou escrever seu primeiro romance em 1936, recebendo inclusive US$ 400 como adiantamento pelo primeiro rascunho de *A crônica dos Wapshot*, chamado então de *The Holy Tree* [A árvore sagrada]. Insatisfeito com o resultado, antes de chegar à editora o jovem Cheever atirou o manuscrito numa lixeira na estação de trem e esqueceu a ideia até a morte de sua mãe, em 1956.

Naquela época, já havia publicado cerca de cem contos em *The New Yorker* e *The New Republic*, mas muitos críticos não lhe davam o merecido reconhecimento. Pode-se chamar de escritor alguém que não tem um romance nas livrarias? O caso é que *A crônica dos Wapshot* tentou abafar os rumores, que não fizeram mais que mudar de forma, já que foram muitos os que achavam que Cheever, na verdade, jamais poderia se livrar de seus contos.

Antes de se deixar dominar pelo álcool, escreveu pelo menos outra centena de contos, nos quais explorou algumas de suas obsessões: o deslocamento em relação à própria existência, a traição feminina, as camadas de gordura do sonho americano, o absurdo do cotidiano numa sociedade que se olha no espelho e não se reconhece. Alguns relatos curtos, como "The Swimmer", saíram do papel para se converter numa alegoria cinematográfica (protagonizada por um Burt Lancaster viciado em cloro) ou uma radiografia sem sentido que se esconde atrás das fachadas das urbanizações perfeitas. "Não nasci numa verdadeira classe social, e então decidi me infiltrar na classe média como espião para atacar de uma posição favorável, mas às vezes esqueço a minha missão e levo o meu disfarce demasiado a sério", disse em certa ocasião o próprio Cheever, que, depois de ganhar o Pulitzer e o National Book Critics Circle Award, vendeu sua alma ao diabo por um relógio de ouro e, como se não fosse mais do que um de seus personagens, acabou estrelando um anúncio da marca Rolex enquanto seus contos reunidos apareciam na revista *Cosmopolitan* nas mãos de uma modelo de maiô.

LAURA FERNÁNDEZ

APRESENTAÇÃO DO CONTO
The Swimmer

No dia em que Neddy Merrill decidiu voltar para casa nadando, todo mundo se lembrava de ter bebido demais na noite anterior. E ainda que da borda da piscina dos Westerhazy as nuvens parecessem construir, a distância, uma cidade fantasma que poderia se chamar Hackensack, a ideia lhe pareceu excelente. Neddy, personagem exemplar do lado amável do sonho americano, percorreria a nado, cruzando as piscinas de seus vizinhos, os 12 km que separavam a mansão dos Westerhazy da sua e, uma vez ali, encontraria suas quatro filhas jogando tênis no jardim e anunciaria que havia criado uma nova rota de volta para casa à qual daria o nome de rio Lucinda, em homenagem a sua mulher. Então ela sorriria, prepararia um martini para ele e os dois deixariam que a tarde se extinguisse no reflexo de sua própria piscina. Decidido a conquistar uma rota tão exclusiva quanto delirante, Neddy mergulha na piscina dos Westerhazy, a atravessa e, com a sensação de estar fazendo o que de melhor se pode fazer num dia perfeito de final de verão, pula a cerca e cruza a pé a distância que o separa do jardim dos vizinhos, que o convidam a tomar um trago antes de continuar sua missão.

E tudo seria perfeito se o tempo não brincasse conosco.

Porque, à medida que avança em seu trajeto, o dia de verão se converte num terrível e frio dia de inverno e os vizinhos começam a tratar Neddy como se sempre tivesse sido um louco solitário. Mas quem é Neddy Merrill? É mesmo casado? Ainda mora em Bullet Park? Por que diabos está atravessando o condado a nado? E por que está nu? O pesadelo americano está servido.

Publicado originalmente em 16 de julho de 1964 na prestigiosa revista *The New Yorker*, "The Swimmer" não é apenas a melhor maneira de se entrar no universo de Cheever (sempre foi considerado o seu melhor conto, pois resume como nenhum outro o que seu autor quis nos dizer e que poderia ser algo como "Algo cheira mal no sonho americano"), mas também o mais acessível e apaixonante de seus contos. Sua leitura resulta tão cristalina como as águas das piscinas em que o torturado Neddy Merrill mergulha. Tudo ocorre de forma cronológica, e assim o desenvolvimento da ação é quase o de um conto de fadas maldito. Um sujeito tem uma ideia excelente num maravilhoso dia de verão e seu sonho acaba por devorá-lo.

Cronista das sombras do apodrecido *American way of life*, Cheever assistiu à queda do pano de fundo do sonho americano e converteu o desencanto no mote de sua narrativa, que, para muitos, nunca pôde se livrar do disfarce de conto. "Um conto é aquilo que você diz a si mesmo na recepção do dentista enquanto espera que lhe arranquem um molar. É um bálsamo eficaz para a dor. Quem lê contos? Gosto de pensar que são homens e mulheres em salas de espera, homens e mulheres que buscam compreender uns aos outros e entender o mundo confuso que nos rodeia", disse em certa ocasião, convencido de que histórias como as de Neddy Merrill podem ser uma espécie de acalanto sem data de validade.

LAURA FERNÁNDEZ

The Swimmer

It was one of those midsummer Sundays when everyone sits around saying, "I *drank* too much last night." You might have heard it whispered[1] by the parishioners[2] leaving church, heard it from the lips of the priest himself, struggling with his cassock[3] in the *vestiarium*[4], heard it from the golf links[5] and the tennis courts, heard it from the wildlife preserve[6] where the leader of the Audubon group was suffering from a terrible hangover[7]. "I *drank* too much," said Donald Westerhazy. "We all *drank* too much," said Lucinda Merrill. "It must have been the wine," said Helen Westerhazy. "I *drank* too much of that claret[8]."

This was at the edge[9] of the Westerhazys' pool[10]. The pool, fed[11] by an artesian well[12] with a high iron content, was a pale shade of green[13]. It was a fine day. In the west there was a massive stand of cumulus cloud[14] so like a city seen from a distance—from the bow[15] of an approaching ship—that it might have had a name. Lisbon. Hackensack. The sun was hot. Neddy Merrill sat by the green water, one hand in it,

1 **whispered:** sussurrado • 2 **parishioners:** paroquianos • 3 **struggling with his cassock:** brigando com sua batina • 4 ***vestiarium*:** vestiário • 5 **golf links:** campos de golfe • 6 **wildlife preserve:** reserva florestal e animal • 7 **hangover:** ressaca • 8 **claret:** clarete (vinho) • 9 **edge:** beira • 10 **pool:** piscina • 11 **fed:** alimentada • 12 **artesian well:** poço artesiano • 13 **a pale shade of green:** cor verde-clara • 14 **a massive stand of cumulus cloud:** um grupo enorme de nuvens brancas e baixas • 15 **bow:** proa

one around a glass of gin. He was a slender[1] man—he seemed to have the especial slenderness of youth—and while he was far from young he had slid down his banister[2] that morning and given the bronze backside[3] of Aphrodite on the hall table a smack[4], as he jogged toward[5] the smell of coffee in his dining room. He might have been compared to a summer's day, particularly the last hours of one, and while he lacked[6] a tennis racket or a sail bag[7] the impression was definitely one of youth, sport, and clement weather. He had been swimming and now he was breathing deeply, stertorously[8] as if he could gulp into his lungs[9] the components of that moment, the heat of the sun, the intenseness of his pleasure. It all seemed to flow into his chest. His own house stood in Bullet Park[10], eight miles to the south, where his four beautiful daughters would have had their lunch and might be playing tennis. Then it occurred to him that by taking a dogleg[11] to the southwest he could reach his home by water.

His life was not confining[12] and the delight[13] he took in this observation could not be explained by its suggestion of escape. He seemed to see, with a cartographer's eye, that string[14] of swimming pools, that quasi-subterranean stream[15] that curved across the county[16]. He had made a discovery,

1 **slender:** magro • 2 **he had slid down his banister:** havia deslizado da sua varanda • 3 **backside:** traseiro • 4 **a smack:** tapa • 5 **as he jogged toward:** enquanto corria em direção a • 6 **he lacked:** lhe faltasse • 7 **sail bag:** bolsa de navegação • 8 **stertorously:** ruidosamente • 9 **gulp into his lungs:** encher os pulmões com • 10 **his own house stood in Bullet Park:** sua própria casa ficava em Bullet Park • 11 **a dogleg:** curva fechada • 12 **confining:** limitada • 13 **delight:** prazer • 14 **string:** cadeia, sucessão • 15 **stream:** riacho • 16 **that curved across the county:** que desenhava uma curva pelo condado

a contribution to modern geography; he would name the stream Lucinda after his wife[1]. He was not a practical joker[2] nor was he a fool but he was determinedly original and had a vague and modest idea of himself as a legendary figure. The day was beautiful and it seemed to him that a long swim might enlarge and celebrate its beauty.

He took off a sweater that was hung over his shoulders[3] and dove in[4]. He had an inexplicable contempt[5] for men who did not hurl themselves into pools[6]. He swam a choppy crawl[7], breathing either with every stroke[8] or every fourth stroke and counting somewhere well in the back of his mind the one-two one-two of a flutter kick[9]. It was not a serviceable[10] stroke for long distances but the domestication of swimming had saddled the sport with[11] some customs and in his part of the world a crawl was customary[12]. To be embraced and sustained by the light green water was less a pleasure, it seemed, than the resumption[13] of a natural condition, and he would have liked to swim without trunks[14], but this was not possible, considering his project. He hoisted himself up on the far curb[15]—he never used the ladder[16]—and started across the

1 **he would name the stream Lucinda after his wife:** ele daria ao riacho o nome de Lucinda em homenagem a sua esposa • 2 **practical joker:** piadista • 3 **he took off a sweater that was hung over his shoulders:** tirou o pulôver que levava sobre os ombros • 4 **dove in:** mergulhou • 5 **contempt:** desprezo • 6 **hurl themselves into pools:** se atiravam decididamente nas piscinas • 7 **choppy crawl:** nado crawl não sincronizado, irregular • 8 **stroke:** braçada • 9 **flutter kick:** batida de perna do nado crawl • 10 **serviceable:** prática • 11 **the domestications of swimming had saddled the sport with:** a utilização doméstica da natação havia marcado esse esporte com • 12 **customary:** habitual • 13 **resumption:** retomada • 14 **trunks:** sunga • 15 **he hoisted himself up on the far curb:** se obrigou a sair pela beirada do outro lado • 16 **ladder:** escada

lawn[1]. When Lucinda asked where he was going he said he was going to swim home.

The only maps and charts he had to go by were remembered or imaginary but these were clear enough. First there were the Grahams[2], the Hammers, the Lears, the Howlands, and the Crosscups. He would cross Ditmar Street to the Bunkers and come, after a short portage[3], to the Levys, the Welchers, and the public pool in Lancaster. Then there were the Hallorans, the Sachses, the Biswangers, Shirley Adams, the Gilmartins, and the Clydes. The day was lovely, and that he lived in a world so generously supplied with water seemed like a clemency, a beneficence. His heart was high and he ran across the grass. Making his way home by an uncommon route gave him the feeling that he was a pilgrim[4], an explorer, a man with a destiny, and he knew that he would find friends all along the way; friends would line the banks of the Lucinda River[5].

He went through a hedge[6] that separated the Westerhazys' land[7] from the Grahams', walked under some flowering apple trees, passed the shed that housed their pump and filter[8], and came out at the Grahams' pool. "Why, Neddy,[9]" Mrs. Graham said, "what a marvelous surprise. I've been trying to get

1 **lawn:** gramado • 2 **the Grahams:** os Graham (em inglês, para referir-se a uma família ou a uma linhagem, usa-se o sobrenome no plural) • 3 **after a short portage:** depois de uma rápida parada • 4 **pilgrim:** peregrino • 5 **friends would line the banks of the Lucinda River:** os amigos demarcariam as margens do rio Lucinda • 6 **hedge:** cerca viva • 7 **the Westerhazys' land:**a propriedade dos Westerhazys (se o sobrenome termina em -s, o apóstrofo do possessivo é colocado ao final da palavra) • 8 **the shed that housed their pump and filter:** o galpão onde guardavam a bomba e o filtro • 9 **why, Neddy:** ora, Neddy

you on the phone all morning. Here, let me get you a drink." He saw then, like any explorer, that the hospitable customs and traditions of the natives would have to be handled with diplomacy if he was ever going to reach his destination. He did not want to mystify[1] or seem rude[2] to the Grahams nor did he have the time to linger there[3]. He swam the length[4] of their pool and joined them in the sun and was rescued, a few minutes later, by the arrival of two carloads of friends[5] from Connecticut. During the uproarious reunions[6] he was able to slip away[7]. He went down by the front of the Grahams' house, stepped over a thorny[8] hedge, and crossed a vacant lot[9] to the Hammers'. Mrs. Hammer, looking up from her roses, saw him swim by although she wasn't quite sure who it was. The Lears heard him splashing[10] past the open windows of their living room. The Howlands and the Crosscups were away. After leaving the Howlands' he crossed Ditmar Street and started for[11] the Bunkers', where he could hear, even at that distance, the noise of a party.

The water refracted the sound of voices and laughter and seemed to suspend it in midair[12]. The Bunkers' pool was on a rise[13] and he climbed some stairs to a terrace where twenty-five or thirty men and women were drinking. The only person in the water was Rusty Towers, who floated there on a

1 **to mystify:** desconcertar • 2 **or seem rude:** ou parecer rude • 3 **nor did he have time to linger there:** nem tinha tempo para se demorar ali • 4 **the length:** comprimento • 5 **two carloads of friends:** dois carros cheios de amigos • 6 **the uproarious reunions:** os efusivos e barulhentos encontros • 7 **to slip away:** escapulir • 8 **thorny:** espinhoso • 9 **a vacant lot:** terreno baldio • 10 **splashing:** respingando • 11 **started for:** se pôs em marcha até • 12 **in midair:** no ar • 13 **on a rise:** numa elevação

rubber raft[1]. Oh, how bonny and lush were the banks of the Lucinda River[2]! Prosperous men and women gathered by the sapphire-colored waters[3] while caterer's men[4] in white coats passed them cold gin. Overhead a red de Haviland trainer[5] was circling around and around and around in the sky with something like the glee of a child in a swing[6]. Ned felt a passing affection[7] for the scene, a tenderness[8] for the gathering, as if it was something he might touch. In the distance he heard thunder[9]. As soon as Enid Bunker saw him she began to scream: "Oh, look who's here! What a marvelous surprise! When Lucinda said that you couldn't come I thought I'd *die*." She made her way to him through the crowd[10], and when they had finished kissing she led him to the bar[11], a progress that was slowed by the fact that he stopped to kiss eight or ten other women and shake the hands of as many men. A smiling bartender[12] he had seen at a hundred parties gave him a gin and tonic and he stood by the bar for a moment, anxious not to get stuck[13] in any conversation that would delay[14] his voyage. When he seemed about to[15] be surrounded he dove in and swam close to the side to avoid colliding[16]

1 **a rubber raft:** um bote de borracha • 2 **how bonny and lush were the banks of the Lucinda River!:** como eram bonitas e exuberantes as margens do rio Lucinda! • 3 **gathered by the sapphire-colored waters:** reunidos juntos às águas da cor das safiras • 4 **the caterer's men:** os empregados do serviço de bufê • 5 **a red de Haviland trainer:** um avião de treino de Haviland vermelho • 6 **the glee of a child in a swing:** a felicidade de uma criança num balanço • 7 **a passing affection:** um carinho passageiro • 8 **tenderness:** ternura • 9 **thunder:** trovão • 10 **crowd:** multidão • 11 **she led him to the bar:** o levou até o bar • 12 **bartender:** garçom • 13 **to get stuck:** ficar preso • 14 **that would delay:** que pudesse atrasar • 15 **about to:** prestes a • 16 **to avoid colliding:** para evitar colidir

with Rusty's raft. At the far end of the pool he bypassed[1] the Tomlinsons with a broad smile[2] and jogged up the garden path[3]. The gravel[4] cut his feet but this was the only unpleasantness[5]. The party was confined to the pool, and as he went toward the house he heard the brilliant, watery sound of voices fade[6], heard the noise of a radio from the Bunkers' kitchen, where someone was listening to a ballgame[7]. Sunday afternoon. He made his way through the parked cars and down the grassy border of their driveway[8] to Alewives' Lane. He did not want to be seen on the road in his bathing trunks but there was no traffic and he made the short distance to the Levys' driveway, marked with a private property sign and a green tube for the *New York Times*[9]. All the doors and windows of the big house were open but there were no signs of life; not even a dog barked[10]. He went around the side of the house to the pool and saw that the Levys had only recently left. Glasses and bottles and dishes of nuts were on a table at the deep end, where there was a bathhouse or gazebo[11], hung with Japanese lanterns[12]. After swimming the pool he got himself a glass and poured a drink. It was his fourth or fifth drink and he had swum nearly half the length of the Lucinda River. He felt tired, clean, and pleased at that moment to be alone; pleased with everything.

1 **he bypassed:** cruzou com • 2 **with a broad smile:** com um amplo sorriso • 3 **jogged up the garden path:** subiu correndo pelo caminho do jardim • 4 **gravel:** cascalho • 5 **unpleasantness:** desagradável • 6 **fade:** se apagarem • 7 **ballgame:** partida de beisebol • 8 **the grassy border of the driveway:** a margem coberta de erva do caminho de entrada • 9 **a green tube for the *New York Times*:** tubo verde para colocar o jornal quando está chovendo (no caso, a família recebia o *New York Times*) • 10 **not even a dog barked:** nem sequer um cão latia • 11 **gazebo:** belvedere, pequena construção em jardins de onde se tem uma vista agradável • 12 **lanterns:** lanternas

It would storm. The stand of cumulus cloud—that city—had risen and darkened, and while he sat there he heard the percussiveness of thunder again. The de Haviland trainer was still circling overhead and it seemed to Ned that he could almost hear the pilot laugh with pleasure in the afternoon; but when there was another peal of thunder[1] he took off for home[2]. A train whistle blew[3] and he wondered what time it had gotten to be[4]. Four? Five? He thought of the provincial station at that hour, where a waiter, his tuxedo concealed by a raincoat[5], a dwarf[6] with some flowers wrapped[7] in newspaper, and a woman who had been crying would be waiting for the local[8]. It was suddenly growing dark; it was that moment when the pin-headed[9] birds seem to organize their song into some acute[10] and knowledgeable recognition of the storm's approach. Then there was a fine noise of rushing water from the crown of an oak[11] at his back, as if a spigot[12] there had been turned. Then the noise of fountains came from the crowns of all the tall trees. Why did he love storms, what was the meaning of his excitement when the door sprang open[13] and the rain wind fled rudely up the stairs[14], why had the simple task of shutting the windows of an old house seemed fitting[15] and urgent, why did the first watery notes of

1 **peal of thunder:** trovão • 2 **he took off for home:** ele foi para casa • 3 **a train whistle blew:** ouviu-se o apito de um trem • 4 **what time it had gotten to be:** que horas deviam ser • 5 **his tuxedo concealed by a raincoat:** seu smoking oculto sob uma capa de chuva • 6 **dwarf:** anão • 7 **wrapped:** envolvidas • 8 **the local:** o trem local • 9 **pin-headed:** de bico largo e cabeça pequena • 10 **acute:** agudo • 11 **the crown of an oak:** a copa de um carvalho • 12 **spigot:** esguicho • 13 **sprang open:** se abria de um golpe • 14 **the rain wind fled rudely up the stairs:** o vento da chuva subia bruscamente pelas escadas • 15 **fitting:** adequada

a storm wind have for him the unmistakable sound of good news, cheer, glad tidings[1]? Then there was an explosion, a smell of cordite[2], and rain lashed[3] the Japanese lanterns that Mrs. Levy had bought in Kyoto the year before last, or was it the year before that?

He stayed in the Levys' gazebo until the storm had passed. The rain had cooled the air and he shivered[4]. The force of the wind had stripped[5] a maple[6] of its red and yellow leaves and scattered[7] them over the grass and the water. Since it was midsummer the tree must be blighted[8], and yet he felt a peculiar sadness at this sign of autumn. He braced his shoulders[9], emptied his glass, and started for the Welchers' pool. This meant crossing the Lindleys' riding ring[10] and he was surprised to find it overgrown with grass and all the jumps dismantled[11]. He wondered if the Lindleys had sold their horses or gone away for the summer and put them out to board[12]. He seemed to remember having heard something about the Lindleys and their horses but the memory[13] was unclear. On he went, barefoot[14] through the wet grass, to the Welchers', where he found their pool was dry.

This breach[15] in his chain of water disappointed him absurdly, and he felt like some explorer who seeks a torrential

1 **glad tidings:** boas notícias • 2 **cordite:** cordite (tipo de pólvora) • 3 **lashed:** fustigava • 4 **he shivered:** tremia de frio • 5 **had stripped:** desfolhou • 6 **a maple:** um bordo • 7 **scattered:** espalhado • 8 **blighted:** afetada por algum parasita • 9 **he braced his shoulders:** firmou os ombros • 10 **riding ring:** picadeiro (lugar onde os domadores adestram os cavalos e onde se aprende a montar) • 11 **the jumps dismantled:** os obstáculos desmontados • 12 **put them out to board:** haviam sido enviados a um estábulo para que fossem cuidados • 13 **the memory:** a lembrança disso • 14 **barefoot:** descalço • 15 **breach:** brecha; interrupção, quebra

headwater[1] and finds a dead stream. He was disappointed and mystified. It was common enough to go away for the summer but no one ever drained[2] his pool. The Welchers had definitely gone away. The pool furniture was folded, stacked, and covered with a tarpaulin[3]. The bathhouse was locked. All the windows of the house were shut, and when he went around to the driveway in front he saw a for-sale sign nailed to a tree[4]. When had he last heard from the Welchers—when, that is, had he and Lucinda last regretted an invitation to dine[5] with them? It seemed only a week or so ago. Was his memory failing or had he so disciplined it in the repression of unpleasant facts that he had damaged his sense of the truth? Then in the distance he heard the sound of a tennis game. This cheered him[6], cleared away all his apprehensions and let him regard the overcast sky[7] and the cold air with indifference. This was the day that Neddy Merrill swam across the county. That was the day! He started off then for his most difficult portage.

Had you gone for a Sunday afternoon ride that day you might have seen him, close to naked[8], standing on the shoulders[9] of route 424, waiting for a chance to cross. You might

1 **headwater:** nascente de rio • 2 **drained:** esvaziava • 3 **the pool furniture was folded, stacked and covered with a tarpaulin:** os móveis da piscina estavam dobrados, empilhados e cobertos por uma lona • 4 **nailed to a tree:** pregado numa árvore • 5 **regretted an invitation to dine:** haviam recusado um convite para jantar • 6 **this cheered him:** isso o deixou de bom humor • 7 **regard the overcast sky:** observar o céu nublado • 8 **close to naked:** quase nu • 9 **shoulders:** acostamento

have wondered if he was the victim of foul play[1], had his car broken down[2], or was he merely a fool[3]. Standing barefoot in the deposits of the highway—beer cans, rags[4], and blowout patches[5]—exposed to all kinds of ridicule, he seemed pitiful[6]. He had known when he started that this was a part of his journey—it had been on his maps—but confronted with[7] the lines of traffic[8], worming through[9] the summery light, he found himself unprepared. He was laughed at, jeered at[10], a beer can[11] was thrown at him, and he had no dignity or humor to bring to the situation. He could have gone back, back to the Westerhazys', where Lucinda would still be sitting in the sun. He had signed nothing, vowed nothing[12], pledged nothing[13], not even to himself. Why, believing as he did, that all human obduracy[14] was susceptible to common sense, was he unable to turn back[15]? Why was he determined to complete his journey even if it meant putting his life in danger? At what point had this prank[16], this joke, this piece of horseplay[17] become serious? He could not go back, he could not even recall[18] with any clearness the green water at the Westerhazys', the sense of inhaling the day's components,

1 **the victim of foul play:** a vítima de um delito • 2 **broken down:** avariado • 3 **merely a fool:** simplesmente um louco • 4 **rags:** trapos • 5 **blowout patches:** restos de pneus remendados • 6 **pitiful:** patético • 7 **confronted with:** confrontado com • 8 **the lines of traffic:** as filas de carros • 9 **worming through:** avançando entre • 10 **jeered at:** ridicularizado • 11 **a beer can:** uma lata de cerveja • 12 **(he had) vowed nothing:** não havia jurado nada • 13 **(he had) pledged nothing:** não havia prometido nada • 14 **obduracy:** obstinação • 15 **to turn back:** voltar atrás • 16 **prank:** brincadeira; travessura • 17 **horseplay:** jogo absurdo • 18 **recall:** lembrar

the friendly and relaxed voices saying that they had *drunk* too much. In the space of an hour, more or less, he had covered a distance that made his return impossible.

An old man, tooling down the highway[1] at fifteen miles an hour, let him get to the middle of the road, where there was a grass divider[2]. Here he was exposed to the ridicule of the northbound[3] traffic, but after ten or fifteen minutes he was able to cross. From here he had only a short walk to the Recreation Center at the edge of the village of Lancaster, where there were some handball courts and a public pool.

The effect of the water on voices, the illusion of brilliance and suspense, was the same here as it had been at the Bunkers' but the sounds here were louder, harsher[4], and more shrill[5], and as soon as he entered the crowded enclosure he was confronted with regimentation[6]. "ALL SWIMMERS MUST TAKE A SHOWER BEFORE USING THE POOL. ALL SWIMMERS MUST USE THE FOOTBATH, ALL SWIMMERS MUST WEAR THEIR IDENTIFICATION DISKS." He took a shower, washed his feet in a cloudy and bitter solution, and made his way to the edge of the water. It stank[7] of chlorine and looked to him like a sink[8]. A pair of lifeguards[9] in a pair of towers blew police whistles at what seemed to be regular intervals and abused the swimmers[10]

1 **tooling down the highway:** dirigindo lentamente pela estrada • 2 **a grass divider:** canteiro • 3 **northbound:** na direção norte • 4 **harsher:** mais ásperos • 5 **more shrill:** mais estridentes • 6 **regimentation:** regulamentação • 7 **it stank:** fedia • 8 **sink:** cano de esgoto • 9 **lifeguards:** salva-vidas • 10 **abused the swimmers:** insultavam os nadadores

through a public address system. Neddy remembered the sapphire water at the Bunkers' with longing[1] and thought that he might contaminate himself—damage his own prosperousness and charm[2]—by swimming in this murk[3], but he reminded himself that he was an explorer, a pilgrim, and that this was merely a stagnant bend[4] in the Lucinda River. He dove, scowling with distaste[5], into the chlorine and had to swim with his head above water to avoid collisions, but even so he was bumped into, splashed, and jostled[6]. When he got to the shallow end[7] both lifeguards were shouting at him: "Hey, you, you without the identification disk, get outa the water." He did, but they had no way of pursuing him[8] and he went through the reek of suntan oil[9], and chlorine out through the hurricane fence[10] and passed the handball courts. By crossing the road he entered the wooded part[11] of the Halloran estate[12]. The woods were not cleared and the footing was treacherous[13] and difficult until he reached the lawn[14] and the clipped beech hedge[15] that encircled their pool.

The Hallorans were friends, an elderly couple of enormous wealth who seemed to bask in the suspicion[16] that they

1 **longing:** saudade • 2 **charm:** encanto • 3 **murk:** água turva • 4 **a stagnant bend:** uma curva com água estagnada • 5 **scowling with distaste:** com uma careta de asco • 6 **he was bumped into, splashed, and jostled:** chocavam-se contra ele, molhavam-no e recebia cotoveladas • 7 **the shallow end:** o lado mais raso da piscina • 8 **no way of pursuing him:** não tinham como persegui-lo • 9 **the reek of suntan oil:** o mau cheiro do bronzeador • 10 **the hurricane fence:** o alambrado • 11 **the wooded part:** a zona arborizada • 12 **estate:** propriedade • 13 **the footing was treacherous:** o caminho era traiçoeiro • 14 **lawn:** gramado • 15 **clipped beech hedge:** cerca viva de faias podadas • 16 **to bask in the suspicion:** se deleitar na suspeita

might be Communists. They were zealous reformers[1] but they were not Communists, and yet when they were accused, as they sometimes were, of subversion, it seemed to gratify and excite them. Their beech hedge was yellow and he guessed this had been blighted like the Levys' maple[2]. He called hullo, hullo[3], to warn the Hallorans of his approach, to palliate his invasion of their privacy. The Hallorans, for reasons that had never been explained to him, did not wear bathing suits. No explanations were in order[4], really. Their nakedness was a detail in their uncompromising zeal for reform and he stepped politely out of his trunks[5] before he went through the opening in the hedge.

Mrs. Halloran, a stout[6] woman with white hair and a serene face, was reading the *Times*. Mr. Halloran was taking beech leaves out of the water with a scoop[7]. They seemed not surprised or displeased to see him. Their pool was perhaps the oldest in the county, a fieldstone rectangle, fed by a brook[8]. It had no filter or pump and its waters were the opaque gold of the stream.

"I'm swimming across the county," Ned said.

"Why, I didn't know one could[9]," exclaimed Mrs. Halloran.

"Well, I've made it from the Westerhazys'[10]," Ned said. "That must be about four miles."

1 **zealous reformers:** reformistas entusiastas • 2 **maple:** bordo • 3 **hullo:** forma alternativa de escrever *hello* • 4 **no explanations were in order:** não era necessário explicar nada • 5 **he stepped politely out of his trunks:** tirou educadamente sua sunga • 6 **stout:** robusta • 7 **scoop:** pá • 8 **brook:** riacho • 9 **why, I didn't know one could:** Imagine, eu não sabia que alguém conseguiria fazer • 10 **I've made it from the Westerhazys':** estou vindo desde a casa dos Westerhazys

He left his trunks at the deep end, walked to the shallow end, and swam this stretch. As he was pulling himself out of the water he heard Mrs. Halloran say, "We've been *terribly* sorry to hear about all your misfortunes[1], Neddy."

"My misfortunes?" Ned asked. "I don't know what you mean."

"Why, we heard that you'd sold the house and that your poor children . . . "

"I don't recall having sold the house," Ned said, "and the girls are at home."

"Yes," Mrs. Halloran sighed[2]. "Yes . . . " Her voice filled the air with an unseasonable melancholy and Ned spoke briskly[3]. "Thank you for the swim."

"Well, have a nice trip," said Mrs. Halloran.

Beyond the hedge he pulled on his trunks and fastened[4] them. They were loose[5] and he wondered if, during the space of an afternoon, he could have lost some weight. He was cold and he was tired and the naked Hallorans and their dark water had depressed him. The swim was too much for his strength but how could he have guessed this, sliding down the banister that morning and sitting in the Westerhazys' sun? His arms were lame[6]. His legs felt rubbery[7] and ached at the joints[8]. The worst of it was the cold in his bones and the feeling that he might never be warm again. Leaves were falling down around him and he smelled woodsmoke on the wind. Who would be burning wood at this time of year?

1 **misfortunes:** desgraças • 2 **sighed:** suspirou • 3 **briskly:** energicamente • 4 **fastened:** o ajeitou • 5 **they were loose:** estava folgado • 6 **lame:** rígidos • 7 **his legs felt rubbery:** suas pernas pareciam de borracha • 8 **ached at the joints:** suas articulações doíam

He needed a drink. Whiskey would warm him, pick him up[1], carry him through the last of his journey, refresh his feeling that it was original and valorous to swim across the county. Channel swimmers[2] took brandy. He needed a stimulant. He crossed the lawn in front of the Hallorans' house and went down a little path to where they had built a house, for their only daughter, Helen, and her husband, Eric Sachs. The Sachses' pool was small and he found Helen and her husband there.

"Oh, *Neddy*, " Helen said. "Did you lunch at Mother's?"

"Not *really*, " Ned said. "I *did* stop to see your parents." This seemed to be explanation enough. "I'm terribly sorry to break in on you[3] like this but I've taken a chill[4] and I wonder if you'd give me a drink."

"Why, I'd *love* to," Helen said, "but there hasn't been anything in this house to drink since Eric's operation. That was three years ago."

Was he losing his memory, had his gift[5] for concealing painful facts let him forget that he had sold his house, that his children were in trouble, and that his friend had been ill? His eyes slipped[6] from Eric's face to his abdomen, where he saw three pale, sutured scars[7], two of them at least a foot[8] long. Gone was his navel[9], and what, Neddy thought, would

1 **pick him up:** reanimá-lo • 2 **Channel swimmers:** nadadores de grandes distâncias • 3 **to break in on you:** interrompê-lo • 4 **I've taken a chill:** senti um calafrio • 5 **gift:** dom • 6 **slipped:** deslizaram • 7 **pale, sutured scars:** cicatrizes pálidas de suturas • 8 **a foot long:** com cerca de 30 cm (1 pé = 30,48 cm) • 9 **gone was his navel:** seu umbigo havia desaparecido

the roving hand[1], bed-checking one's gifts at 3 A.M.[2], make of a belly with no navel, no link to birth, this breach[3] in the succession?

"I'm sure you can get a drink at the Biswangers'," Helen said. "They're having an enormous do[4]. You can hear it from here. Listen!"

She raised her head and from across the road, the lawns, the gardens, the woods, the fields, he heard again the brilliant noise of voices over water. "Well, I'll get wet," he said, still feeling that he had no freedom of choice about his means of travel[5]. He dove into the Sachses' cold water and, gasping[6], close to drowning[7], made his way from one end of the pool to the other. "Lucinda and I want *terribly* to see you[8]," he said over his shoulder, his face set toward the Biswangers'. "We're sorry it's been so long and we'll call you *very* soon."

He crossed some fields to the Biswangers' and the sounds of revelry[9] there. They would be honored to give him a drink, they would be happy to give him a drink. The Biswangers invited him and Lucinda for dinner four times a year, six weeks in advance. They were always rebuffed[10] and yet they continued to send out their invitations, unwilling to comprehend the rigid and undemocratic realities of their

1 **roving hand:** mão errante • 2 **bed-checking one's gifts at 3 a.m.:** explorando seu próprio corpo às 3 da madrugada • 3 **breach:** brecha • 4 **an enormous do:** uma grande festa • 5 **means of travel:** meios de transporte • 6 **gasping:** respirando com dificuldade • 7 **close to drowning:** quase se afogando • 8 **Lucinda and I want terribly to see you:** Lucinda e eu queremos muito vê-los • 9 **revelry:** farra • 10 **rebuffed:** recusados

society. They were the sort of people who discussed the price of things at cocktails, exchanged market tips[1] during dinner, and after dinner told dirty stories[2] to mixed company. They did not belong to Neddy's set[3]—they were not even on Lucinda's Christmas card list[4]. He went toward their pool with feelings of indifference, charity, and some unease[5], since it seemed to be getting dark and these were the longest days of the year. The party when he joined it was noisy and large. Grace Biswanger was the kind of hostess who asked[6] the optometrist, the veterinarian, the real-estate dealer[7], and the dentist. No one was swimming and the twilight[8], reflected on the water of the pool, had a wintry gleam[9]. There was a bar and he started for this. When Grace Biswanger saw him she came toward him, not affectionately as he had every right to expect, but bellicosely.

"Why, this party has everything," she said loudly, "including a gate crasher[10]."

She could not deal him a social blow[11]—there was no question about this and he did not flinch[12]. "As a gate crasher," he asked politely, "do I rate a drink[13]?"

"Suit yourself[14]," she said. "You don't seem to pay much attention to invitations."

1 **market tips:** dicas da Bolsa • 2 **dirty stories:** histórias sujas • 3 **set:** círculo social • 4 **not even on Lucinda's Christmas card list:** nem mesmo na lista de cartões de Natal de Lucinda • 5 **unease:** mal-estar • 6 **the kind of hostess who asked:** o tipo de anfitriã que convidava • 7 **real-estate dealer:** corretor de imóveis • 8 **twilight:** crepúsculo • 9 **wintry gleam:** brilho invernal • 10 **gate crasher:** penetra • 11 **blow:** golpe • 12 **he did not flinch:** não se alterou • 13 **do I rate a drink?:** tenho direito a um drinque? • 14 **suit yourself:** sirva-se

She turned her back on him[1] and joined some guests, and he went to the bar and ordered a whiskey. The bartender served him but he served him rudely. His was a world in which the caterer's men kept the social score[2], and to be rebuffed[3] by a part-time barkeep meant that be had suffered some loss of social esteem[4]. Or perhaps the man was new and uninformed. Then he heard Grace at his back say: "They went for broke overnight[5]—nothing but income—and he showed up drunk[6] one Sunday and asked us to loan[7] him five thousand dollars. . . ." She was always talking about money. It was worse than eating your peas off a knife. He dove into the pool, swam its length and went away.

The next pool on his list, the last but two, belonged to his old mistress[8], Shirley Adams. If he had suffered any injuries at the Biswangers' they would be cured here. Love—sexual roughhouse[9] in fact—was the supreme elixir, the pain killer, the brightly colored pill that would put the spring back into his step[10], the joy of life in his heart. They had had an affair last week, last month, last year. He couldn't remember, It was he who had broken it off[11], his was the upper hand[12],

1 **she turned her back on him:** ela lhe deu as costas • 2 **the caterer's men kept the social score:** os empregados do bufê sabiam quem era quem • 3 **to be rebuffed:** ser menosprezado • 4 **social esteem:** apreço social • 5 **they went for broke overnight:** eles faliram da noite para o dia • 6 **he showed up drunk:** ele apareceu bêbado • 7 **to loan:** emprestar • 8 **mistress:** amante • 9 **sexual roughhouse:** jogos sexuais violentos • 10 **the brightly colored pill that would put the spring back in his step:** a pílula de cor brilhante que o deixaria como novo • 11 **it was he who had broken it off:** foi ele quem terminou • 12 **his was the upper hand:** era ele quem tinha o controle

and he stepped through[1] the gate of the wall that surrounded her pool with nothing so considered as self-confidence. It seemed in a way to be his pool, as the lover, particularly the illicit lover, enjoys the possessions of his mistress with an authority unknown to holy matrimony[2]. She was there, her hair the color of brass[3], but her figure, at the edge of the lighted, cerulean[4] water, excited in him no profound memories. It had been, he thought, a lighthearted[5] affair, although she had wept[6] when he broke it off. She seemed confused to see him and he wondered if she was still wounded. Would she, God forbid[7], weep again?

"What do you want?" she asked.

"I'm swimming across the county."

"Good Christ[8]. Will you ever grow up?"

"What's the matter?"

"If you've come here for money," she said, "I won't give you another cent."

"You could give me a drink."

"I could but I won't. I'm not alone."

"Well, I'm on my way[9]."

He dove in and swam the pool, but when be tried to haul himself up[10] onto the curb[11] he found that the strength in his arms and shoulders had gone, and he paddled[12] to the ladder and climbed out. Looking over his shoulder he saw,

1 **he stepped through:** passou por • 2 **holy matrimony:** sagrado matrimônio • 3 **brass:** cobre • 4 **cerulean:** cerúlea (de cor azul) • 5 **lighthearted:** divertido • 6 **wept:** chorado • 7 **God forbid:** que Deus não permita • 8 **Good Christ:** Deus meu • 9 **well, I'm on my way:** bom, vou indo • 10 **to haul himself up:** subir • 11 **curb:** beirada • 12 **he paddled:** chapinhou

in the lighted bathhouse, a young man. Going out onto the dark lawn he smelled chrysanthemums or marigolds[1]—some stubborn autumnal fragrance—on the night air, strong as gas. Looking overhead he saw that the stars had come out, but why should he seem to see Andromeda, Cepheus, and Cassiopeia? What had become of the constellations of midsummer? He began to cry.

It was probably the first time in his adult life that he had ever cried, certainly the first time in his life that he had ever felt so miserable, cold, tired, and bewildered[2]. He could not understand the rudeness[3] of the caterer's barkeep or the rudeness of a mistress who had come to him on her knees[4] and showered his trousers with tears. He had swum too long, he had been immersed too long, and his nose and his throat[5] were sore[6] from the water. What he needed then was a drink, some company, and some clean, dry clothes, and while he could have cut directly across the road to his home he went on to the Gilmartins' pool. Here, for the first time in his life, he did not dive but went down the steps into the icy[7] water and swam a hobbled[8] side stroke[9] that he might have learned as a youth. He staggered[10] with fatigue on his way to the Clydes' and paddled the length of their pool, stopping again and again with his hand on the curb to rest. He climbed up

1 **marigold:** calêndulas • 2 **bewildered:** desconcertado • 3 **rudeness:** má educação • 4 **on her knees:** de joelhos • 5 **throat:** garganta • 6 **were sore:** estavam irritados • 7 **icy:** gelada • 8 **hobbled:** tropeçando • 9 **side stroke:** estilo de nadar, de lado, com a cabeça para fora da água, no qual as pernas se movimentam como uma tesoura e são dadas braçadas no estilo peito • 10 **he staggered:** cambaleou

the ladder and wondered if he had the strength to get home. He had done what he wanted, he had swum the county, but he was so stupefied with exhaustion[1] that his triumph seemed vague. Stooped[2], holding on to the gateposts[3] for support, he turned up the driveway of his own house.

The place was dark. Was it so late that they had all gone to bed? Had Lucinda stayed at the Westerhazys' for supper? Had the girls joined her there or gone someplace else? Hadn't they agreed, as they usually did on Sunday, to regret all their invitations and stay at home? He tried the garage doors to see what cars were in but the doors were locked[4] and rust came off the handles[5] onto his hands. Going toward the house, he saw that the force of the thunderstorm had knocked one of the rain gutters loose[6]. It hung down over the front door like an umbrella rib[7], but it could be fixed in the morning. The house was locked, and he thought that the stupid cook[8] or the stupid maid[9] must have locked the place up until he remembered that it had been some time since they had employed a maid or a cook. He shouted, pounded on the door[10], tried to force it with his shoulder, and then, looking in at the windows, saw that the place was empty.

1 **stupefied with exhaustion:** aturdido pela exaustão • 2 **stooped:** encurvado • 3 **holding on to the gateposts:** agarrando-se aos postes • 4 **locked:** trancadas • 5 **rust came off the handles:** a ferrugem se soltava das maçanetas • 6 **had knocked one of the rain gutters loose:** uma das canaletas para a água da chuva havia se soltado • 7 **umbrella rib:** vareta de sombrinha • 8 **cook:** cozinheiro(a) • 9 **maid:** arrumadeira • 10 **pounded on the door:** bateu na porta

1ª edição fevereiro de 2011 | **Diagramação** Patrícia De Michelis
Fonte Bembo e Berthold Akzidenz Grotesk | **Papel** Chamois 75g/m²
Impressão e acabamento Yangraf